PARDON ME

The saloon was bursting at the seams. Every table was filled. The bar was lined from end to end. Women flitted about, being as friendly as they could be.

With a start, Fargo realized that few of the females were white. Most were Flatheads, but a few were from other tribes. He went to skirt a table when suddenly a man in a chair pushed back and stepped directly into his path. They bumped shoulders, hard.

"Watch where you're going, damn you," the man complained.

Fargo went on by, saying, "You walked into me, lunkhead." He was brought up short by a hand on his arm.

"What did you just call me?" The man was compact and muscular and had the shoulders of a bull.

"Want me to spell it?" Fargo tore loose and took another step, only to have his arm grabbed a second time. He turned, just as a fist arced at his face. . . .

THE TRAILSMAN

#321

FLATHEAD FURY

by

Jon Sharpe

A SIGNET BOOK

SIGNET
Published by New American Library, a division of
Penguin Group (USA) Inc., 375 Hudson Street,
New York, New York 10014, USA
Penguin Group (Canada), 90 Eglinton Avenue East, Suite 700, Toronto,
Ontario M4P 2Y3, Canada (a division of Pearson Penguin Canada Inc.)
Penguin Books Ltd., 80 Strand, London WC2R 0RL, England
Penguin Ireland, 25 St. Stephen's Green, Dublin 2,
Ireland (a division of Penguin Books Ltd.)
Penguin Group (Australia), 250 Camberwell Road, Camberwell, Victoria 3124,
Australia (a division of Pearson Australia Group Pty. Ltd.)
Penguin Books India Pvt. Ltd., 11 Community Centre, Panchsheel Park,
New Delhi - 110 017, India
Penguin Group (NZ), 67 Apollo Drive, Rosedale, North Shore 0632,
New Zealand (a division of Pearson New Zealand Ltd.)
Penguin Books (South Africa) (Pty.) Ltd., 24 Sturdee Avenue,
Rosebank, Johannesburg 2196, South Africa

Penguin Books Ltd., Registered Offices:
80 Strand, London WC2R 0RL, England

First published by Signet, an imprint of New American Library,
a division of Penguin Group (USA) Inc.

First Printing, July 2008
10 9 8 7 6 5 4 3 2 1

The first chapter of this book previously appeared in *Oregon Outrage*, the
three hundred twentieth volume in this series.

PUBLISHER'S NOTE
This is a work of fiction. Names, characters, places, and incidents either are
the product of the author's imagination or are used fictitiously, and any resem-
blance to actual persons, living or dead, events, or locales is entirely
coincidental.

The publisher does not have any control over and does not assume any
responsibility for author or third-party Web sites or their content.

The Trailsman

Beginnings . . . they bend the tree and they mark the man. Skye Fargo was born when he was eighteen. Terror was his midwife, vengeance his first cry. Killing spawned Skye Fargo, ruthless, cold-blooded murder. Out of the acrid smoke of gunpowder still hanging in the air, he rose, cried out a promise never forgotten.

The Trailsman they began to call him all across the West: searcher, scout, hunter, the man who could see where others only looked, his skills for hire but not his soul, the man who lived each day to the fullest, yet trailed each tomorrow. Skye Fargo, the Trailsman, the seeker who could take the wildness of a land and the wanting of a woman and make them his own.

Flathead Lake, 1861—where the poison of hate destroyed innocent lives.

1

The rider came down out of the high country and drew rein on the crest of a low hill. Below stretched a long, broad valley. Mission Valley, some called it. Beyond, to the north, gleamed Flathead Lake, the largest body of water between the Mississippi River and the Pacific Ocean.

The rider's handsome face was burned brown by the relentless sun. He was tall in height and broad of shoulder, and sat his saddle as someone long accustomed to being on horseback. In addition to buckskins, he wore a white hat turned brown with dust, and a red bandanna. On his hip was a well-used Colt. In the scabbard on his saddle nestled a Henry rifle.

The splendid stallion he rode was often referred to as a pinto. A closer look revealed that the markings were different; the dark spots were smaller, and there were more of them. To those who knew horses, his was more properly called an Ovaro or Overo. But pinto would do.

The heat of the summer's day had brought sweat to the rider and his mount. The man removed his hat, swiped at his perspiring face with a sleeve, then jammed his hat back on and pulled the brim low. He was about to gig the Ovaro down the slope when movement drew his attention to a procession moving out of the hills.

The rider's eyes, which were the same vivid blue as the lake miles away, narrowed. Four men on horseback were strung out in single file. Trailing them were three shuffling figures in dresses, and unless the rider's eyes were playing tricks on him, the three women had their arms bound behind their backs and were linked one to the other by rope looped around their necks.

"It is worth a look-see," the man said to the Ovaro, and tapped his spurs. When he was still a ways off, one of the four men spotted him, and shouted and pointed. The party promptly halted. Two of the men moved their mounts to either side of the women.

The stockiest of the bunch came out and waited with the butt of his rifle on his leg and his finger on the trigger. He wore seedy clothes more common on the riverfront than in the mountains. On his left hip was a bowie. "That will be far enough, mister!" he called out when the tall rider had but ten yards to cover. "What do you want?"

The tall man drew rein and leaned on his saddle horn. "Nothing in particular," he answered. "You are the first people I have come across in over a week."

The stocky riverman's dark eyes raked the other from dusty hat to dusty boots. "Mind if I ask your handle?"

"Skye Fargo."

"I am called Kutler." The man paused. "Haven't I heard of you somewhere? Something about a shooting match you won? Or was it that you scout for the army?"

"Both," Fargo said. He noticed that the other three men had their hands near their revolvers.

"What are you doing in this neck of the woods? Army work?" Kutler asked with more than a hint of suspicion.

Fargo shook his head. "I have time to myself and wanted to get away by my lonesome for a while," he lied. He gazed to the north. "The last time I was through this area, the only settlement had a handful of cabins and a lean-to and called itself Polson."

"Polson is still there, but near a hundred people call it home these days," Kutler unwittingly confirmed the

2

intelligence passed on to Fargo by the army. "By the end of next year, that number will be a thousand."

"Did you just say a thousand?" Fargo grinned. "Do you have a flask hid somewhere?"

Kutler chuckled. "I do sound drunk, don't I? But I am as sober as can be. Not by choice, mind you. The man I work for has his rules. He is the one predicting there will be that many."

"He is awful optimistic," Fargo said. It was true more and more people were flocking west each year, but Mission Valley and Flathead Lake were so far north, it would be decades yet before the influx rivaled that of, say, Denver or Cheyenne.

"Big Mike Durn has reason to be. He has it all worked out. If he says there will be a thousand, I believe him."

Fargo told his second lie. "I have heard of him but I can't remember where." The colonel had told him about Durn.

"No doubt you have," Kutler said. "Big Mike got his start running keelboats on the Mississippi. He became famous when he was in a tavern brawl and killed three men with his bare fists. Self-defense, the jury said. It was in all the newspapers."

"So he is *that* Big Mike," Fargo said as if impressed.

"The one and only," Kutler said proudly. "The scourge of the Mississippi, they used to call him. But he had to leave the river and wound up here."

Fargo studied the women. Indian women, they were, and not one had seen twenty winters. All three wore finely crafted doeskin dresses and moccasins.

"That was six months ago," Kutler was saying. "Now Big Mike pretty much runs Polson as he pleases."

Indicating the women, Fargo asked, "How do they fit in?"

"Their fathers or husbands borrowed money from Big Mike and can't repay him, so these squaws have to work off the debt."

Fargo was about to ask how when the man behind Kutler gave a harsh bark of impatience.

"Damn it, Kutler, how much longer are you two going to jaw? I want to get back. Another day without whiskey and my insides will shrivel." He was a small man with a hooked beak of a nose, a scar on his pointed chin, and a perpetual scowl. Like Fargo, he wore buckskins. Cradled in his left arm was a Sharps. A revolver adorned his hip.

Kutler glanced sharply over his shoulder. "That will be enough out of you, Tork. Big Mike put me in charge. We will ride on when I say we ride on."

Tork looked at the two men who were on either side of the women and made a show of rolling his eyes.

Fargo saw Kutler's hand drift toward his revolver, but for whatever reason, Kutler let his hand drop and muttered something under his breath. "Good friends, are you?" Fargo remarked.

Kutler snorted. "Tork doesn't like me and I don't like him. But so long as we both work for Big Mike, nothing much will come of it."

"Why is that?"

"Because if one of us kills the other, Big Mike will kill whoever lives." Kutler lifted his reins. "If you are ever in Polson, look me up. I am usually at the Whiskey Mill."

Fargo had to ask before they rode off. "You say these women are to work off a debt? How do they do that, exactly?"

"How do you think?" Kutler rejoined, with a wink and a leer. "They would run off if they could but we do not give them the chance." He clucked to his horse. "If any of these squaws strike your fancy, they will be at the Whiskey Mill, too."

The women filed past with their heads bowed. Judging by the way they wore their hair and the styles of their dress, two were Flatheads and one was a Coeur d'Alene. The youngest Flathead was quite pretty, with nice lips and full cheeks and beautiful eyes that fixed on Fargo's as she went by in what he took to be mute appeal.

"Get along there!" snapped one of her guards.

Fargo sat and watched them until they were stick figures. "Hell," he said to the Ovaro. His gaze drifted to the range of mountains to the northwest. Several of the peaks were so high, they were mantled with snow all year long. If he wanted to be by his lonesome, that was the place to go.

Fargo reined toward the lake. He held to a walk. There was no hurry, and the Ovaro was tired. The image of the pretty Flathead seemed to float in the air before him. "Now I have even more reason," he said aloud.

Fargo was looking forward to a hot meal, a bottle of whiskey, and a card game. He must remember to keep his ears pricked. As his friend, Colonel Travis, had made plain the night before Fargo left the fort: "Your orders are to find out if the rumors are true. If they are, get word to me, and I will take whatever measures I deem necessary. Unfortunately, since this is largely a civilian matter, I must be careful how I proceed or the newspapers will be clamoring for my hide."

Fargo had said that he understood.

"I wouldn't ask this of you but there is no one else I trust half as much as I trust you," Colonel Travis remarked. "But be careful. Don't get involved if you can help it."

"I will try my best not to," Fargo had responded.

Now, with the sun well past its apex, Fargo reckoned he would reach Polson about twilight. He came on an isolated cabin, and shortly after, a second homestead. They were not there the last time he was here, and each brought a frown of disapproval.

The West was growing too damn fast for his liking.

Fargo rounded a bend and suddenly had to rein up to avoid riding into an old man in shabby homespun who was staggering down the middle of the trail, a nearly empty whiskey bottle clutched in his bony hand. "Watch where you are going, old-timer."

The man stopped and swayed, peering up at Fargo through bloodshot eyes. Taking a swig, he testily demanded, "What are you trying to do? Ride me down?" He was so drunk he slurred every syllable.

"If you don't want to be trod on, you shouldn't hog the trail."

Sniffing in resentment, the old man put his spindly arms on his bony hips. He wore a Colt Navy in a scuffed holster but he made no attempt to draw it. "For your information, I am almost out of bug juice and I am on my way into Polson for more."

"I reckon you have had enough," Fargo mentioned.

"What makes you say that, you busybody?"

"You are going the wrong way."

The old man gave a start. "How's that?"

"Polson is to the north. You are walking south."

"The hell you say!" The oldster glanced about him in bewilderment, then cackled and exclaimed, "I'll be damned! Somehow or other I got turned around."

"I wonder how," Fargo said drily.

The old man smiled and held out a hand. His teeth, the few that were left, were yellow. "Thaddeus Thompson, sir. Thank you for pointing out my mistake."

Fargo bent down. It was like shaking hands with dry bones. "It will be dark soon. Maybe you should go home."

"And not get my refill?" Thaddeus took a step back in indignation. "How do you expect me to make it through the night? When I am sober the nightmares are worse."

"Why would a gent your age have nightmares?"

Thaddeus grew even more indignant. "What does my age have to do with anything, you ornery pup? I have nightmares for the same reason anyone does. Because things happened that seared my soul. Because in the dark of night, the dead haunt us."

"For a drunk you have a way with words," Fargo complimented him.

Sorrowfully hanging his head, Thaddeus said, "They blame me, so they come back to remind me."

"Who does?"

"My wife, Martha, and my brother, Simon. They were murdered and there was nothing I could do." Thaddeus upended the last of his whiskey into his mouth, then uttered a low sob.

"Someone killed them?"

"I swear, you do not have enough brains to grease a pan. Isn't that what I just said? But I don't have proof so there is not much I can do."

"I would like to hear about it," Fargo said.

"Go to hell. It hurts too much. It is bad enough Martha and Simon crawl out of their graves at night to point fingers at me." Wheeling, Thaddeus staggered in the direction of Polson, swinging the now empty bottle by its neck.

Fargo kneed the Ovaro and came up next to him. "How about if we ride double? You will reach the settlement a lot sooner."

"When I get there, I get there," Thaddeus declared. "I would not go at all if I did not need more gut-warmer."

"It is a long walk," Fargo tried again.

"I am no infant. Kindly take you and your horse elsewhere so I can suffer in silence."

"I am in no hurry."

The sun was poised on the rim of the world. Soon only a golden crown remained. Then that, too, was gone. The sky gradually darkened, giving birth to stars, which multiplied like rabbits.

Thaddeus Thompson had been plodding along mumbling to himself, but he abruptly jerked his head up and wagged a finger at Fargo. "I thought I told you to mosey on. I do not need your company."

"It isn't smart to be out alone at night," Fargo observed. "The Blackfeet have been acting up of late. And there are grizzlies hereabouts."

"Hell, the Blackfeet have held a grudge since Lewis and Clark. As for the silvertips, most stay up in the mountains these days. To come down here is an invite to be stuffed and mounted."

"So the answer is no?"

"If your head were any harder, you would have rock between your ears."

Fargo had taken all of the old man's barbs he was going to. "And you called me ornery, you old goat. Have it your way," he said, and applied his spurs. But no sooner did he do so than the undergrowth parted and onto the trail strode the lord of the Rockies, the very creature Fargo had been concerned about. "Son of a bitch!" he exclaimed, drawing rein.

Apparently Thaddeus had not noticed the newcomer because he asked, "What has you in a dither, sonny?"

Fargo did not have to answer. The grizzly did it for him by rearing onto its hind legs, tilting its head, and growling.

2

Grizzlies were living mountains of muscle with razor teeth and claws. Immensely strong, they could rip a man apart with one swipe of an enormous paw. They were unpredictable; nine times out of ten they ran at the sight or smell of a human being, but the tenth time was to be dreaded, for stopping a griz was next to impossible. Their skulls were so thick, the bone was virtual armor. To hit the heart or a lung was almost as difficult owing to their huge bodies.

But that did not stop Fargo from yanking the Henry from his saddle scabbard. Levering a round into the chamber, he pressed the stock to his shoulder, saying quietly to Thaddeus Thompson, "Don't move."

The old man did not heed. Flapping his arms, he walked toward the bear, bawling, "Go away! Shoo! Bother someone else, you consarned nuisance!"

Fargo braced for a charge. He would do what he could but he doubted he could bring the grizzly down before it reached Thompson and reduced him to a pile of shattered bones and ruptured flesh. "Stop, damn it," Fargo hollered.

Thaddeus glanced back, and laughed. "Don't shoot! It's only old One Ear. He has been around nearly as long as I have."

Fargo looked, and sure enough, the bear did appear to be past its prime. Splashes of gray marked the muzzle, and it was more gaunt than a grizzly should be. The left ear was missing, apparently torn off, leaving a ridge of scar tissue. But Fargo did not lower the Henry. An old bear was still dangerous. "It might attack," he warned.

Thaddeus Thompson dismissed the notion with a wave. "Shows how much you know! One Ear never hurt anybody. He comes and goes as he pleases, and hardly anyone ever sees him except me. I think he likes me."

"You are an idiot," Fargo said.

"Think so, do you? Just you watch!" Thaddeus squared his thin shoulders and boldly marched toward the bear, saying as if greeting a long-lost friend, "How do you do, One Ear? How have you been? If you drank coffin varnish I would share mine if I had any left."

Then and there Fargo decided the old-timer was more than a few bales short of a wagon load. He took a bead on the grizzly's chest.

One Ear was regarding the old man as if it could not quite make up its mind what to do. Suddenly the bear dropped onto all fours, ponderously wheeled, and crashed off into the underbrush. Within moments the racket faded and the woods were still.

"See?" Thaddeus gloated. "I told you he wouldn't hurt me."

Fargo waited to be good and sure the bear was gone, then let down the Henry's hammer, slid the rifle into the scabbard, and gigged the Ovaro up next to Thompson. "You will get yourself killed one day pulling that stunt."

"We all end up in a grave."

"So?" Fargo said.

"So when my time comes, I would rather it was quick than slow. One Ear is better than lying abed for a month of Sundays, wasting away."

Fargo had to admit the old man had a point but he still said, "A bear can be messy. A bullet to the brain would not hurt as much."

"Shoot myself? Hell, boy, if I could, I would. But I

don't have the sand. If I did, Martha and Simon would still be breathing." Thaddeus resumed walking, his head hung low.

"You keep bringing them up," Fargo mentioned. "What happened, if you don't mind telling?"

"It was Martha," Thaddeus said. "She wouldn't keep quiet. She wasn't one of those who look down their nose at Indians just because they are different from us."

"You have lost me."

"Don't your ears work? Martha was heartbroke at how the Indians were being treated. Some of our best friends are red, and it tore her apart to see them abused, and to hear all the talk of wiping them out."

"Who would want to wipe out the Indians?"

"Who else?" Thaddeus retorted. "Big Mike Durn, as they call him. He hates Indians. He thinks the only good one is a dead one." He stopped and stabbed a finger at Fargo. "How about you, mister? Are you a red-hater?"

"I have lived with the Sioux and other tribes," Fargo revealed. "They are not the evil many whites make them out to be. They are people, like us."

Thaddeus showed his yellow teeth again. "A man after my own heart. Maybe I will ride with you, after all."

Fargo almost regretted his offer. The old man had not taken a bath in a coon's age, and to say he stunk was being charitable. Fargo breathed shallow and held his breath when he turned his head to say something. And now that they were friends, Thaddeus was in a talkative mood.

"A word to the wise: When we get to Polson, keep your feelings about Indians to yourself."

"Why?"

"Durn and his men do not take kindly to anyone who speaks well of the red man. Remember my wife? Why, just last week they beat someone for saying as how the Indians had been here first and had as much right to the land as anybody." Thaddeus swore luridly. "That Mike Durn is the meanest cuss who ever drew breath."

"Why doesn't someone do something?"

"It would take a heap of doing. Durn has pretty near twenty tough characters working for him, and they are not shy about getting their way."

"Outlaws?"

"Not strictly, no. But they are as bad a bunch as I ever saw. They will beat a man as soon as look at him."

The situation sounded worse than Fargo had been told. "What about Polson's law-abiding citizens? Why don't they drive him out if it is as bad as you say?"

"Hell, mister. Most are married, and some have kids. Sally Brook stood up to Durn a month ago at the general store. Let him have a piece of her mind, she did, and for that, she was pushed around a bit by Tork and Grunge."

"I have met Tork," Fargo said, and briefly related his run-in.

"He is one of the worst of the bunch, a weasel of a back-shooter who only picks on those weaker than him. The other one you met, Kutler, is what you might call Durn's second-in-command."

"And Grunge?" Fargo asked.

"A freak of nature, is what he is. Grunge is not much bigger than you but he has hands the size of hams. He can break a door with one punch, or cave in a man's face."

Fargo was mentally filing the information. He had learned a lot but there was a lot more yet to uncover. "Old-timer, mind if I ask you a question?"

"I thought that was what you have been doing."

"It is about your wife and brother—"

"About how they died?" Thaddeus broke in. "I would rather not talk about it. But this once I will make an exception." He drew a deep breath. "Durn dropped a tree on them."

"What?"

"Are you hard of hearing? A week 'after Martha gave Durn a piece of her mind, I went off to hunt. Simon was chopping a tree for firewood. He waved as I rode off. That was the last I saw him or my Martha alive."

"But what makes you think Durn was involved?"

"Let me finish. I got back about sundown and found both of them lying under the tree Simon had been chopping. They were crushed to bits."

"The tree might have fallen on them." Fargo had heard of similar mishaps in his travels.

"That is what Durn wants everyone to believe. But I know better. I found a bump on the back of Martha's head."

Fargo shifted in the saddle, and forgot to hold his breath. "You just said a tree fell on her. There were bound to be bumps."

"The tree didn't fall on her *head*. It fell on her chest. After someone knocked her out and laid her and my brother right where the tree would land on top of them."

"Did your brother have a bump on his head?"

Thaddeus took exception. "Are you trying to rile me? No, he did not, but I am willing to bet my bottom dollar he was stabbed."

"You saw a knife wound?"

"I think there was one," Thaddeus said uncertainly. "It was hard to tell. The tree made a mess of him."

Fargo was skeptical. It seemed to him that the old man was blaming Durn for what might have been a simple accident. He made a remark to that effect.

"That is how Durn does it. He kills quietly, and smartly, so he isn't ever blamed."

"I don't know," Fargo said. In his capacity as an investigator for the army, it was important he stick to the facts and not make the mistake of believing others without proof.

"So much for us being friends," Thaddeus grumbled. "Mike Durn has you hoodwinked, and you haven't even met him yet."

"I will soon enough."

Thaddeus fell silent, leaving Fargo to his thoughts. Although he did not mind helping the army out, it was not his usual line of work. But Colonel Travis was a friend, and he would do what he could.

The situation was compounded by the fact that Polson was so far removed from civilization. Normally, the town marshal or county sheriff would handle things, but Polson did not have a marshal and was not in an established county. For that matter, Polson was not part of a state, either. It was in Nebraska Territory, which stretched from the Canadian border to the north clear down to Kansas Territory in the south.

Not that the legal niceties mattered all that much. Since the federal government was trying to set up an Indian reservation, and rumors had filtered back of an organized effort to prevent it by driving the Indians out, the problem was clearly under federal jurisdiction.

So Colonel Travis decided to send in a special investigator.

Enter Fargo.

The sun relinquished its reign to the gathering twilight.

As Fargo had reckoned, by then he was within sight of Polson and the south shore of Flathead Lake.

"I hate coming here," Thaddeus Thompson remarked. "It makes me think of Martha, and how she met her end."

"Did anyone take a look at the bodies besides you?" Fargo asked.

"I never thought to ask. I dug the remains out from under the tree and buried them. Then I came here and accused Mike Durn to his face."

"What did he do?"

"He called me a loon, and most folks believed him."

"Most?"

"A few still have their backbones. Sally Brook took my side but she is only one gal and there is not much she can do."

14

"How would I go about finding her?"

"Sally runs a shop for ladies. She sells dresses and hats and such. You can find her there most any hour of the day."

As they neared the lights of Polson, Fargo recollected more of the local geography. The settlement had been built in a sort of natural amphitheater at the south end of the lake, which fed into the nearby Flathead River. To the west towered the Mission Mountains.

The last time Fargo was here, the nights were quiet and peaceful, the few residents, homebodies who turned in early so they could be up at the crack of dawn. Those days, and nights, were gone.

Now, Polson had the trappings of a boomtown. Nearly every building was ablaze with light. Piano music wafted on the breeze, punctuated by loud voices and laughter. Every hitch rail was filled. Coarse men in dirty clothes prowled the street, admiring women in tight dresses who sashayed about advertising their wares.

"I'll be damned," Fargo said.

"Not what you expected, huh?" Thaddeus said glumly. "Every cutthroat and no-account in the territory has heard Polson is a haven for their kind. This is only the beginning."

Fargo was going to ask what he meant but just then a drunk came stumbling out of the shadows and nearly collided with the Ovaro.

"I know him!" Thaddeus declared, and awkwardly slid off, nearly tripping over his own feet. "Fred! It's me!"

"Thaddeus?"

"What do you say to sharing that bottle?"

Fred beamed and clapped Thaddeus on the back, and the pair melted into the shadows.

Fargo rode on down the street. The most noise came from the largest and newest building. A sign out front proclaimed that he had found the Whiskey Mill.

Since there was no room at the hitch rail, he drew up at a corner of the overhang and tied the reins to the post.

Sliding the Henry from the scabbard, Fargo stepped to the batwings. A blast of sound and odors hit him: curses, squeals, mirth, the tinkle of poker chips, the rattle of a roulette wheel, the smell of beer and whiskey mixed with cigar smoke and perfume.

Fargo breathed deep, and pushed on in. The saloon was bursting at the seams. Every table was filled. The bar was lined from end to end. Women flitted about, being as friendly as they could be.

With a start, Fargo realized that few of the females were white. Most were Flatheads, but a few were from other tribes. He went to skirt a table when suddenly a man in a chair pushed back and stepped directly into his path. They bumped shoulders, hard.

"Watch where you are going, damn you," the man complained.

Fargo went on by, saying, "You walked into me, lunkhead." He was brought up short by a hand on his arm.

"What did you just call me?" The man was compact and muscular and had the shoulders of a bull.

"Want me to spell it?" Fargo tore loose and took another step, only to have his arm grabbed a second time. He turned, just as a fist arced at his face.

3

Fargo sidestepped and the fist missed his cheek by a whisker. Before the man could recover his balance, Fargo slammed the Henry's stock against his head. It rocked the man onto his boot heels but he did not go down. With a bellow that drew the attention of those around them, he drove a fist at Fargo's gut. Again Fargo used the Henry, flicking it so that the man's fist connected with the barrel and not his body. The man howled and shook his hand, then feinted with his other fist while kicking at Fargo's groin. Twisting, Fargo took the kick on the outside of his thigh.

The man was red with rage and drink, and Fargo was mad, himself. Stepping back, he struck the Henry against the man's left knee. That brought a roar of pain and the man doubled over, clutching his leg and exposing the back of his head. Fargo brought the stock sweeping down and the man groaned and pitched to the floor, unconscious.

Fargo slowly lowered the Henry. He had half a mind to kick the bastard's ribs in. Instead, he turned and found himself the center of attention. The saloon had gone quiet and nearly everyone was staring at him. Ignoring them, he strode on. People scampered aside to let him pass. Those at the bar parted to give him space.

The hothead had done Fargo a favor. Now he was someone to be reckoned with. Word would spread, and be exaggerated in the telling, and by tomorrow

17

everyone in Polson would take him for a bad man. That could work to his advantage.

No sooner did the thought cross his mind than all those around him were giving him even more room. Not because of what he had done but because a knot of four men were coming toward him from the back. Fargo watched them in the mirror while saying to the bartender, "A bottle of your best. And if you have watered it down, God help you."

Two of the four men Fargo had already met: Kutler and Tork. The third had to be the man called Grunge. He was about Fargo's size but his hands were incredibly huge, three times as big as normal hands would be, and his knuckles were walnuts.

The fourth man had to be Big Mike Durn. He stood head and shoulders above everyone else. His chest was immense. From what Fargo had heard, he expected Durn to be an unkempt river rat. But Durn was clean-shaven and freshly scrubbed, his suit immaculate. He did not wear a hat. Nor, to Fargo's surprise, did he wear a revolver—that Fargo could see. Durn's eyes were a steely gray, and when he smiled, as he did now, the smile did not touch them. "That was nicely done, Mr. Fargo."

Fargo arched an eyebrow.

"Kutler told me about running into you," Big Mike said. "You are everything the gossips claim."

"A man shouldn't listen to biddy hens," Fargo said.

Durn leaned an elbow on the bar. "Welcome to my saloon. To my town. To what will one day be my territory."

Fargo glanced at him, and damn if the man wasn't serious. "I seem to recollect that Polson was here long before you showed up."

"That it was," Mike Durn said. "But there was no one in charge. No top dog, if you will."

"And there is now?"

"You are looking at him."

"I admire your modesty," Fargo said as the bartender placed a bottle and a glass in front of him.

Durn laughed, but the laughter was as cold as his smile. "Modesty is for the weak, for those too timid to reach out and take what they want from life. I am not timid."

Fargo opened the bottle and filled his glass. "Care to wet your throat?" he asked.

"Don't mind if I do," Durn said. All he had to do was crook a finger at the bartender, and a glass was in front of him. He smiled as Fargo poured. "I am obliged. Usually I limit myself to two drinks a night, but for you I will make an exception."

"You never get drunk?" Fargo had never met a riverman who did not like to drown himself in liquor.

"Not anymore, no. A man in my position cannot afford to be weak when there are those who would tear him down."

"You seem fond of that word," Fargo noted. "Weak."

Big Mike Durn tipped the glass to his mouth but took only a sip. "There are two kinds of people in this world. The strong and the weak. The wolves and the sheep. Most people are sheep. They do what they are told and abide by the law from the cradle to the grave. They are nobodies while they live, and no one remembers them after they die." He set down the glass. "That is not for me. I am a wolf. I take what I want when I want. I wrest what I need from those that have it, and bury them if they get in my way. I have taken over this town, and in another couple of years I will take over the entire territory."

Fargo smothered a smirk. The man sure was fond of himself. "The United States government might have a say about that," he remarked.

"Oh, I have no doubt they will try to stop me," Durn said somberly. "It would not surprise me if reports have already reached them, and they have sent someone to check on those reports." He paused. "Say you, for instance."

It took every iota of self-control Fargo had not to betray his surprise. Whatever else Big Mike Durn might be, he was not stupid. "I work for the army from time to time," he admitted. "But as a scout, nothing more."

"So I have heard," Durn said. "But I wonder. Some might call it a coincidence, you showing up here, but I am not a big believer in coincidence. Convince me I am wrong and I will allow you to stay."

Fargo had a sharp retort on the tip of his tongue, but he did not say it. He suddenly noticed that the other three had spread out and were ringing him, Kutler with his hand on his bowie, Tork with the Sharps casually pointed in his general direction, and Grunge with those enormous fists of his balled. "How do I go about doing that?"

"I leave that to you," Durn said. "But I will grant you one night in Polson. Entertain yourself as you see fit, and if you want to stay longer, come see me in the morning and persuade me to let you stay."

"I do not like being told what to do."

"That makes two of us." Durn smiled, and was about to walk off when a shout rose to the rafters.

"You, there! The son of a bitch who bloodied me!"

Fargo looked in the mirror. He had forgotten about the jackass who took a swing at him. The man was on his feet, swaying slightly, blood trickling down his cheek, his teeth bared in a snarl. "Go bother someone else," Fargo said.

"Like hell!" The man was poised to draw, his fingers inches above his revolver. "Turn and face me! Or so help me, I will shoot you in the back."

Big Mike Durn sighed. "That will be enough out of you, Everett. Be smart for once and go sleep it off."

"Stay out of this!" Everett snapped. "You saw what he did to me. I have the right to repay the favor."

"You have whatever rights I say you have," Durn said quietly. "One of the rights you do *not* have is the right not to do whatever I tell you to do. I will say it one more time. Go sleep the booze off. In the morning look me up and apologize."

By now the saloon had gone quiet again, with all present waiting to see the outcome.

Everett gestured, but not with his gun arm. "I swear. The airs you put on. You might have the rest of these yacks afraid but not me. I will do as I please, and it pleases me to kill this son of a bitch."

Tork had shifted and was pointing the Sharps at Everett. "Let me take care of this peckerwood, Mr. Durn."

"No. That buffalo gun of yours would splatter his brains all over," Big Mike said.

"How about me, then?" Kutler offered, starting to draw his bowie.

"Open him up with that big pigsticker and he will get blood on the floor," Durn said. "No, I would rather that Grunge do the honors."

Everett was staring at them as if he could not believe what he was hearing. "I am standing right here!" he declared. "No one is a laying hand on me, do you hear?"

"Not a hand so much as a sledge," Durn said, and bobbed his head at the man with the enormous fists. "He is yours. Try not to make too much of a mess or you will clean it up."

Fargo saw it all.

Everett swore and grabbed at his six-shooter. His fingers had not quite reached it when Grunge reached him and swept both giant fists up and in. The double crunch was loud enough to be heard clear across the room.

Everett howled and covered his shattered ears with his hands. He bent slightly, enough that Grunge brought his fists smashing down on top of Everett's head. Instead of a crunch there was a thump, and Everett was belly down on the floor, and did not move.

"Now get him out of my sight," Big Mike Durn said gruffly. "And if you break a few of his bones while doing it, so much the better."

Grunge and Tork were quick to obey, each taking an

arm and dragging Everett out. Laughter and insults were flung at the unconscious man by some in the crowd.

Fargo observed that some did not laugh or poke fun. Durn's high-handed methods were not appreciated by everyone. He downed the whiskey in his glass at a gulp and set the glass down.

"I did not take you for the squeamish type," Mike Durn said.

Refilling his glass, Fargo was aware that Kutler had come up on the other side of him. They were slick as grease, this bunch. "I am thirsty, is all."

"Now where were we?" Big Mike said. "Oh. Yes. I was saying as how I suspect you are working for the army. But I hear tell that you claim you came all this way to have some time to yourself."

"What is unusual about that?"

"Nothing. Except that you had the whole Rockies to choose from, and they run from Canada to Mexico. Yet you picked our neck of the woods."

"You have a suspicious nature," Fargo said.

"As suspicious as they come," Mike Durn confirmed. "It is why I have lived as long as I have."

"What is this I hear about a thousand people moving to Polson by the end of next year?" Fargo casually inquired.

"Who told you that?" Durn snapped, and glanced at Kutler, who averted his gaze. "Some people can't help wagging their tongues, it seems. Yes, I am counting on a lot more folks wanting to live here after I have made a few changes."

"Changes how?"

Durn's grin was no grin at all; it was a vicious sneer. "You have yet to convince me you are not a danger to me and my plans. Until you do—" He shrugged, then finished his drink. "It has been interesting. We will talk again tomorrow if you are still here. If you aren't, I will take that as a sign you were lying, and if I ever hear of you anywhere in Polson or Mission Valley, I will send Kutler and Tork and Grunge to talk to you, along with a few others."

"Was that a threat?"

"No. A promise." Big Mike Durn walked off with Kutler in his wake. Three more men fell into step behind them.

Fargo had not counted on this. That sharpshooting contest in Missouri a while back, along with a few other incidents, had brought him notoriety he could do without. Now, most everyone who heard of him knew that he scouted for the army on occasion. He refilled his glass. How in hell was he to convince Durn he was not working for the government when he only had his own say-so? Durn would never accept his word. He might as well ride out by morning. Sure, he could ask around, like the army wanted, but word was bound to reach Durn, and he would be up to his neck in curly wolves out to blow windows in his skull.

"Damn," Fargo said to himself. He decided to find an empty chair and sit in on a card game. That would take his mind off his problem for a while. Picking up the bottle and glass, he pivoted.

Just then a commotion broke out at the batwings. Two men were blocking the doorway to prevent someone from forcing their way through.

"Let go of me, consarn you!" a woman's voice demanded. "I insist on seeing your boss!" The woman tried to shove them out of her way.

Patrons were stopping what they were doing to stare.

Fargo glimpsed lustrous blond hair and a shapely figure, and then the onlookers were making space for Big Mike Durn. Durn gestured, and the two men at the batwings stepped aside to admit the woman.

"Sally, Sally, Sally," Durn said with a smile. "The Whiskey Mill is no fit place for a lady. What are you doing here?"

Fargo had it, then. This was Sally Brook, the woman Thaddeus had told him about.

She put her hands on her hips, her emerald eyes flashing. "Not fit for a lady?" she repeated, and bobbed her head at a Flathead maiden. "Then why are she and these others here?"

"Don't start," Durn said.

"You do not seem to understand," Sally Brook declared. "I will not rest until you stop using these women for your private gain. It is despicable."

"My customers don't think so."

"I just heard that three more were brought in today," Sally said. "Young ones, too."

"The younger, the better," Durn told her. "They are more popular than toothless hags."

"You have no shame, do you?" Sally Brook said, her tone laced with condemnation.

"None whatsoever. But fortunately for you, I have a lot of patience. Otherwise, you would not still be in my good graces."

"I will have to remedy that," Sally Brook said. And before anyone could guess her intent, she stepped up close to Big Mike Durn and slapped him across the face.

4

Skye Fargo half expected Mike Durn to knock Sally Brook to the floor. Apparently, judging by the expressions of those around him, he was not the only one.

As for Durn, he started to raise his right fist, then lowered his arm, took a step back, and laughed. "You always did have more gall than sense. Want to do the other cheek? Here. I will make it easy for you." Durn turned his head.

Sally Brook was furious. "There you go again. Making light of me. But I will not give up. I will do whatever it takes to stop you from mistreating these Indians."

"I have been meaning to ask," Durn said. "Why make all this fuss over a bunch of squaws?"

"They are *people*, confound you! Living, breathing human beings. Not animals. Not savages. Not *squaws*."

"You didn't answer the question."

Sally regarded Mike Durn almost sadly. "I pity you. I truly do. You have no regard for the feelings of others. No concept of what you are doing."

"Like hell," Durn said. "I have everything planned out. I know exactly what I am doing."

"That is not what I meant." Sally suddenly turned toward the maidens. "I know some of you can speak enough English to get by. Listen to me. What this man has you doing is wrong. It is degrading. He has no right to force you to parade yourself."

"They don't do anything a white dove wouldn't do," Big Mike said.

"Walk out!" Sally urged them. "All of you, together. Now. I will see that you get back safely to your families."

Some of the Indian women swapped troubled glances but none of them said anything.

Durn's amusement faded. "That is enough out of you. I will not have you filling their heads with contrary notions. I do not force them to come work for me. They do it to pay off debts."

"I am not that gullible," Sally Brook said.

Durn turned and pointed at several men, all Indians, who were playing poker or faro or roulette. "Look for yourself. I don't force anyone to come here. I don't force them to gamble. They do it of their own free will." He shrugged. "I can't help it if they lose all they have and can't make good."

"You set out honey to catch flies and then claim it is not your fault when they get stuck," Sally said.

Durn looked about the room at all the players and drinkers. "Did you hear her, gentlemen? You are all a bunch of flies."

Hoots of laughter filled the saloon. Sally Brook reddened, then wheeled and stalked out, pushing one of Durn's men out of her way. Kutler started after her but Durn said, "Where do you think you are going? Leave her be. She is harmless." He walked toward the back, his underlings at his heels.

Fargo did not waste a moment. The night air was bracing after the smoke of the saloon. He glanced up and down the street but did not see her. Then a shapely form in a dress passed a house with a lit window, her hair glowing golden. He hurried after her, his spurs jingling, and she heard him, and spun.

"That is far enough, whoever you are. Go back and tell your boss I will not be mistreated."

"I don't work for Mike Durn," Fargo said.

"Then what do you want?"

"To talk to you. We have a common interest. Is there somewhere we can go to be alone?"

"What do you take me for? I don't know you. I have never set eyes on you before. And you want to be alone with me?"

"I am not out to do you harm."

"So you say. But a woman can't be too trusting these days." Sally shook her blond mane. "If you really need to talk, visit me tomorrow at my shop."

Reluctantly, Fargo watched her walk off. He headed back to the saloon. Next to it was a general store, which was closed and dark, and as he was passing the gap between them, he heard the sounds of a scuffle and a woman's voice, pleading, coming from the rear. Instantly, he darted into the gap and ran the length of the buildings.

The back door to the saloon was open. Bathed in the rectangle of light that spilled out were two husky men and a Flathead woman struggling to break free of their grasp. Her back was to Fargo, so all he could see was long black hair and her doeskin dress.

"—back inside and change clothes, squaw," one of the men was saying. "You will do as you are told or we will take a switch to you."

The woman struggled harder but they were too strong for her. They began to haul her toward the door and she dug in her heels.

"Damned wildcat," the other man complained. "Quit it, or I will sock you on the jaw."

"No bruises that anyone can see, remember?" the first man said.

In three bounds Fargo was behind them with the Colt out. He slammed it against the back of the head of the man on the right, shifted, and slammed it against the head of the man on the left. Both crumpled, but he hit them again to ensure they stayed out. Then he turned to the woman.

Only she wasn't there.

She was bolting.

Fargo ran after her but it was soon apparent that barring a miracle, he could forget catching her. She was a two-legged deer, bounding smoothly and lithely, and god-awful fast. He poured on more speed yet gained only a little. "Wait!" he called, but not too loudly. "I only want to talk to you!"

She looked back, her face a blur, and momentarily slowed, breaking stride. In doing so, she tripped and nearly fell.

The mistake cost her.

Fargo launched himself through the air and tackled her about the shins. He tried not to hurt her by bringing her down on top of him. For that he nearly lost an eye when she raked at his face, her fingers hooked like claws. Jerking back, he grabbed her wrists.

"Stop it! I am not your enemy."

Her long hair had fallen over her face and Fargo could not get a good look at her. He tried to grab her chin but she pushed his arm away and kicked and bucked to break free.

The only way to keep her still was to pin her. Suddenly rolling, Fargo covered her body with his and pressed her arms to the ground. She was breathing heavily, and he was aware her dress had hiked above her knees.

"Will you behave?" Fargo requested. He had grown warm all over, and felt a stirring, low down. "I only want to talk."

"Get off me," she said in perfect English.

"Not until you give me your word you will not run off."

She puffed at her hair and some if it fell away, revealing a face as lovely as a sunrise.

"You!" Fargo blurted. It was the young Flathead who had been with Kutler and Tork.

"I remember you," she said, studying him. "You are not one of Dead Heart's men."

"Who?"

"Dead Heart. It is what my people call Mike Durn. His heart is dead to everyone with red skin."

Fargo glanced toward the saloon. The two men still lay where they had fallen but they might come around at any moment. "Do I have your promise you will hear me out?"

"You have it."

Rising, Fargo helped her to stand. Together they hurried half a block to an alley.

"Wait here," Fargo said. "I will be back in a minute with my horse."

"Be quick," she urged.

Fargo sprinted to the end of the alley and out into the street, nearly colliding with a townsman coming the other way. The man swore but did not stop. Slowing so he would not attract attention, Fargo reached the saloon. He untied the Ovaro, forked leather, and rode at a walk back up the street to the alley. When he was sure no one was watching, he reined into it.

His jaw muscles twitched when he did not find the woman where he had left her. "Where are you?" he called out.

"Here." She materialized out of the shadows and held up an arm for him to grab.

Fargo swung her up behind him. "I didn't catch your name."

"Mary Two Trees."

"That is a white name."

"It is the one I was given at the mission. My father is Charlie Two Trees. He stopped using his real name when he took up white ways and began drinking white liquor."

"What do the Flatheads call you?"

"We call ourselves the Salish, not Flatheads. That is another white word. And my Salish name, in your tongue, would be Birds Landing."

Fargo was going to tell her that he knew of many tribes who did not call themselves what the whites called them, but a shout interrupted them.

A portly man in an apron had discovered the unconscious forms behind the saloon. Fortunately, he was on one knee with his back to them.

A jab of his spurs, and Fargo was on his way out of Polson. Birds Landing pressed against him, holding tight. He could feel the swell of her breasts and the contours of her hips. He tried not to dwell on her body as he brought the Ovaro to a canter.

Fargo did not know where he was going. He had not thought that far ahead. "Where do you want me to take you?" he asked. "The mission?" It was a good thirty miles or more south of Polson.

"I live with my people now," Birds Landing said.

"We will go to your village, then."

"That is the first place Durn will have his men look. They would find me and drag me back."

"Your people won't help?"

"Some would, yes. But I do not want Durn mad at them. He hates us enough as it is."

"What about your father?"

"He is the reason I was taken. He likes to gamble. About a moon ago he went to the Whiskey Mill and lost all he had. Durn extended credit to him, and he lost that, too. Since he could not repay the money, Durn took me."

"Durn can't make you work for him against your will."

"My father gave his consent. He was so drunk he could not sit straight, but he marked an X on the paper."

"Durn made him sign a contract?" Fargo had to admire Big Mike's thoroughness. A contract would make it legal, should anyone object. "Have you read the thing?"

"No. It was enough for me to know that I must work for Durn for two years, doing whatever he wants, whenever he wants."

"I am surprised the Salish lets him get away with it."

"My people are trying to avoid trouble with the whites. We have been promised our own reservation, and an Indian agent to help us. If we fight Durn, if we go on the warpath, we stand to lose all we have gained."

Fargo had heard about the reservation. Six years ago or so, a treaty was signed. The government pledged to build a hospital and schools, and to give the Flatheads and two others tribes enough land to live on and all the aid they needed. As was often the case, most of the pledges had not been kept. It did not help matters that some whites resented giving land to the Indians; they would rather drive the Indians off or exterminate them. "Your people are damned if they do and damned if they don't."

"Sorry?"

"They stand to lose no matter what they do," Fargo clarified.

"That is it, exactly."

They rode in silence until Birds Landing cleared her throat. "I told my father I would not work for Durn. That I would not let them take me. So he had them come in the middle of the night when I was asleep. He let them sneak in our lodge and gag and tie me!"

Fargo felt her tremble. "Your own father?"

"It is the whiskey. He is no longer himself. The white man's drink has turned him into someone else."

"The Crows have a saying," Fargo mentioned, "that a Crow who drinks is no longer a Crow."

"Then we are not the only tribe to suffer."

"Far from it," Fargo said.

Her hand rose to his shoulder. "This is far enough. You can stop."

Fargo kept riding. Polson was barely a quarter-mile behind them. "It is not safe yet. Besides, where would you go?"

"I have friends," Birds Landing said. "Perhaps one of them will hide me until Durn stops searching."

"And if he should get his hands on you again?"

"He will have me beaten and withhold food and water until he breaks my spirit. Or, if I still refuse, he will have me thrown into a pit. I have not seen it but I have heard about it, and his beast."

"His what?"

"A creature he keeps hidden. He feeds it the bodies

of those who—" Birds Landing stopped. "Did you hear something?"

Hooves drummed in the darkness behind them. A lot of hooves.

"Damn," Fargo said, and shifted in the saddle just as riders appeared, coming on rapidly.

"They are after us!" Birds Landing exclaimed. "What do we do?"

"Ride like hell," Skye Fargo said.

5

Fargo raced to the west at a gallop. He had complete confidence in the Ovaro's ability to hold its own against any horse, but they had spent most of the day on the trail, and now the stallion was bearing double. Unless he did something, and did it soon, the Ovaro would tire, with dire consequences.

An explosion of shouts warned him their pursuers were flying in heated pursuit.

Birds Landing said urgently in his ear, "Let me off and you will be able to get away."

"No."

"They will catch us if you do not."

"We stick together." Fargo needed to ask her more about Durn and the situation in Mission Valley when he got the chance. "Please stay on," he added to be polite.

"Very well." Birds Landing's mouth brushed his earlobe. "For now I will do as you want."

Then there was no time for small talk. Fargo had to call on all the skill he possessed. They were riding pell-mell at night, across rugged, broken country. At any moment the Ovaro might step into a hole or a rut and go down. Or they might come on a boulder or a log and be unable to avoid it. He must stay alert and focus on riding and only on riding.

His every nerve tingled. Suddenly a dark phalanx appeared ahead: forest. It could be their salvation if they could reach it.

Some of their pursuers were narrowing the gap, and yelling back and forth.

A glance showed Fargo that three riders were rapidly gaining and spreading out as they came so he could not flank them.

Birds Landing's grip tightened. Fargo knew she was afraid they would be caught, afraid of what Durn would do to her. That business about a pit, and a wild beast Durn threw his enemies to—could it be true?

Something swished over their heads and brushed Fargo's shoulder. Another glance showed that one of the riders had closed to within fifteen feet and had thrown a rope, but missed. The man would try again as soon as he had the rope back in his hand.

Suddenly they were in among pines and spruce. Fargo had to slow, but so would they. He had ridden in timber at night before, countless times, and he and the Ovaro moved as one, the stallion responding superbly to the slightest pressure of rein or leg.

A revolver blasted and lead smacked a bole to their right.

"No shooting!" bellowed the deep voice of Big Mike Durn. "I want them alive, damn you!"

Small consolation, Fargo reflected, since he doubted Durn would keep them alive for long. Him, at any rate. The girl was valuable. She had a debt to repay.

A low branch slashed at them out of the ink.

"Duck!" Fargo cried, and did so, feeling Birds Landing shift and press low against his side. They flew under the limb with barely an inch to spare.

Fargo wished the moon was out. Starlight was not enough. They might as well be at the bottom of a well. The thought spawned an idea, and he smiled. It just might work. He urged the Ovaro to go faster, increasing their lead a few yards. The roper had fallen behind; now he and his friends were twenty to thirty feet back.

Could Fargo find what he needed? A thicket would do but they had not come on one yet. Some of the trees had branches low to the ground, but not low enough. Then a small spruce hove out of the night. Only fifteen feet high, it was as broad as it was tall. Fargo swept around it, hauling on the reins as he did, and brought the Ovaro to a standstill so close to the tree, branches were scraping its side.

Heartbeats elapsed, and their three swiftest pursuers flew by on either side. Soon the rest thundered past.

Fargo counted nine, possibly ten. He braced for an outcry but his ruse worked. No one saw them.

One of the last riders was twice the size of the rest. Big Mike Durn chose that moment to shout, "Where did they get to? Don't lose them or there will be hell to pay!"

Gradually, the drum of hooves and the crackle of undergrowth faded.

Fargo didn't linger. Bringing the Ovaro out from behind the spruce, he reined to the northwest. A throaty chuckle reminded him he was not alone.

"You are sly like a fox."

"We were lucky," Fargo said. It could have gone either way. "Where to now? You know this country better than I do. Is there a spot we can camp for the night where Durn isn't likely to find us?"

Birds Landing pondered, then said, "Keep riding. I will direct you."

Night sounds wafted across the valley: the yip of coyotes, the hoot of an owl, the lonesome howl of a wolf. They had covered about a mile when a revolver cracked to the west and was answered by another to the south.

"Why are they shooting?" Birds Landing wondered.

"Signaling," Fargo guessed. "Once they lost us, Durn broke them into groups." That is what he would have done.

"Do you think he suspects you are the one who came to my rescue?"

Fargo couldn't say. But the man who nearly roped them had gotten a good look at the Ovaro, and might describe the stallion to Durn. If Kutler or Tork were along, they would know right away.

"You are a fine rider," Birds Landing remarked. "No warrior in my tribe could do better."

"I have spent half my life in the saddle," Fargo said. Or that was how it seemed.

Now that they were no longer being chased, Fargo was once again aware of the warmth of her body. Her bosom was still pressed flush against him. It made him wonder.

Eventually they came to a series of low hills. Birds Landing guided Fargo up into them until they came to a bench overlooking the valley. The lights of Polson gleamed far off. Even farther away, to the southeast, were a few more. The St. Ignatius Mission, Fargo figured.

At one end of the bench, screened by cottonwoods, was a small spring. The Ovaro wearily hung its head and drank while Fargo stripped off the saddle and saddle blanket. His stomach growled, reminding him he had not eaten all day.

Birds Landing heard. "You are hungry, too?"

"Starved." Fargo could go for an inch-thick steak, or a roast haunch of venison. He settled for opening a saddlebag and taking out a bundle wrapped in rabbit hide. Opening it, he handed a piece of pemmican to Birds Landing. "I have plenty so eat as much as you want." He untied his bedroll, spread out his blankets with his saddle for a pillow, and sank down.

"We are safe here," Birds Landing said.

Fargo helped himself to pemmican. The ground buffalo meat had been mixed with fat and blackberries, and was downright delicious.

Birds Landing accepted another piece and eased down next to him. "Did you make this yourself?"

"I bought it from a Cheyenne woman at a trading post," Fargo revealed. It was rare to find pemmican made with blackberries. Usually chokecherries or other berries were used.

Birds Landing smacked her lips. "You did say I could have as much as I wanted."

"Here." Fargo gave her a handful. As she took them,

her fingers lightly brushed his palm in what might be construed as a caress. Again, Fargo wondered.

Her expression, though, gave no hint of her intentions.

Birds Landing chewed lustily. "For a white man you have been awful nice to me."

"With the body you have, who wouldn't be?" Fargo tested the waters.

Birds Landing blinked, then laughed. "You do not—what is the white saying? Oh, yes. You do not beat around the bush."

"Life is too short for bush-beating," Fargo said, and reaching behind her, pulled her face to his and kissed her full on the lips.

"Oh," Birds Landing said.

Fargo entwined his fingers in her hair and waited for her to make the next move.

"A white woman would slap you now."

"Some would," Fargo agreed. "Some are as miserly with their kisses as they are with their money. Some give their bodies as rewards when their men please them. Some won't ever part their legs because they think it goes against Scripture." Fargo paused. "Then there are those who like to lie with a man as much as they like breathing."

Birds Landing grinned. "That is the most you have said to me since we met. You must like it a lot."

"I am not skittish when it comes to the female body," Fargo teased, and kissed her again, harder, and longer. When he drew back she had a dreamy look about her.

"You kiss as good as you ride." Birds Landing put a hand on his chest and bent to lightly run her tongue along his neck. "And you taste as good as you kiss," she said with a grin.

"How do you taste?" Fargo asked, and molded his mouth to her throat. He nibbled and licked a path to her ear. She squirmed, breathing heavier, and digging her nails into his forearm.

They separated, and Birds Landing rimmed her

mouth with the tip of her tongue. "It is not food I am hungry for now."

"I was hoping you would say that." Fargo moved the bundle of pemmican out of their way and eased her down onto her side, facing him. As he reached for her, she clasped his hand.

"I should stop you. Father DeSmet would say this is wrong."

"I won't tell if you don't," Fargo said, hoping she was not about to change her mind.

"How do they do it?" Birds Landing asked.

"Do what?"

"The priests and the nuns. How do they go their whole lives without? Are they not like the rest of us?"

"You're asking the wrong person," Fargo informed her. "I can't go a week without getting the itch."

Birds Landing laughed merrily. "We are alike, you and I. But for the sake of the priests, while I was at the mission school I did not lift my dress for men, even those from my own tribe."

Fargo playfully hiked at the hem of her doeskin. "How about now? Any lifting allowed?"

"Were it any other white man, I would make Father DeSmet proud and refuse," Birds Landing said. "But I am no longer at the mission, and for you I am willing to do that which he would forbid."

Fargo kissed her again while running his hand up over her thigh to her flat belly, and from there to her breasts. He cupped one, then the other, and pinched her nipples through the dress.

Cooing softly in her throat, Birds Landing ground her bottom against his hardening manhood. She was not timid when it came to lovemaking, as she demonstrated by reaching down and placing her hand on top of his swelling bulge. "You are a stallion," she breathed in his ear.

Fargo couldn't respond, not with the constriction in his throat. He covered her luscious mouth with his and her lips parted to admit his tongue. Hers and his entwined in a silken swirl as her hand commenced to stroke him.

Fargo had to be careful. It would not do to explode before he was ready. He willed himself to ignore her hand and got her dress up around her waist. He caressed each of her thighs in turn, running his fingers from her knees to her nether mound and down again. Her legs were exquisitely smooth to the touch. She arched her back, then pried at his belt to release his member. He nearly gasped when her fingers enfolded him.

Fargo had always been partial to women who liked to do what came naturally to a man and a woman. His appreciation of Birds Landing rose as she cupped him, low down.

Time drifted on a tide of mutual lust. For long minutes there was touching and kissing and the press of hot flesh to hot flesh.

Fargo drowned himself in the feel and the taste of her. When he stroked her slit, she shivered and came up off the blanket as if seeking to take wing. He parted her nether lips, brushed her tiny knob. A few flicks were all it took to drive her into paroxysms of release.

Birds Landing cried out in the Salish tongue. Her fingernails seared his shoulders. Suddenly she clamped her mouth to his neck and bit him so hard, he thought she would draw blood.

"Like it rough, do you?" Fargo said, and plunged the rigid first two fingers of his right hand up into her.

Her mouth parted in a soundless O, and Birds Landing bucked wildly. It was all Fargo could do to keep his fingers inside her. He pumped fast and hard, clear in to the knuckles. Her eyes closed and she clung to him, rhythmically thrusting her bottom to match the tempo of his fingers. It was not long before she crested. Then, spent, she sagged against him.

"It is not over yet," Fargo whispered in her ear. He parted her legs wide, knelt between them, and aligned his throbbing sword with her moist sheath. Her eyes met his, and he rammed into her.

Once again Fargo lost all sense of time. He was aware of his body, of pulsing with pleasure, of Birds Landing squirming and grinding and lavishing wet kisses on every square inch of him her mouth could reach. She reached the pinnacle yet again, her inner walls contracting.

Fargo could no longer hold back. He impaled her, over and over. Her coos and cries became louder, but not so loud that they could be heard far off.

Afterward, Fargo lay on his back, spent but content, and listened for sign of their enemies. All appeared to be tranquil. He started to drift when the crunch of a twig snapped him awake.

Fargo groped for his Colt. Something was out there, and it was stalking them.

6

As quietly as he could, Fargo put himself together. No sounds came out of the encircling cottonwoods but he could not shake the feeling that unseen eyes were watching them. Fully dressed and lying on his side, he bent toward Birds Landing to warn her.

Suddenly a figure in buckskins glided into view, cat-footing stealthily toward them.

Fargo froze, hoping the man would think he was asleep. Then he saw that the stalker had a bow, and spied what could be the top of a quiver poking above the man's right shoulder.

It was an Indian, not a white man.

Since they were in Flathead country, odds were the warrior was a Flathead, or Salish, a member of Birds Landing's tribe. They were on friendly terms with whites but Fargo never took anything for granted. He had his thumb on the Colt's hammer, ready to snap off a shot the moment the warrior raised the bow to unleash a shaft.

That was when Birds Landing stirred and muttered in her sleep in the Salish language.

The warrior stopped. He appeared to be staring intently at Birds Landing. When she did not stir or sit up, he edged forward.

Waiting until the warrior was almost to his saddle, Fargo sprang. The warrior's hand flew to the haft of a tomahawk at his waist but before he could wield it, Fargo was on him. Fargo gave him a hard shove while cocking the Colt and declaring, "Don't move or I will shoot!"

Fargo had no idea if the warrior spoke English. He did not want to kill him, if he could help it. It was bound to stir up trouble, which was the last thing the Flatheads needed, what with the promise of a reservation in the offing.

The warrior fell onto his back and stayed there. He made no attempt to draw the tomahawk or resort to his bow.

Birds Landing sat up with a start. "What is it? What is going on?" Her eyes fastened on the warrior and she exclaimed something in her own language.

The warrior calmly answered.

Rising, Birds Landing said to Fargo, "Do not shoot! He will not harm us."

"How can you be so sure?" Fargo demanded.

"He is my brother."

Fargo slowly holstered the Colt but kept his hand on it as the two Salish warmly embraced and addressed one another in their own language. He waited for Birds Landing to explain what her brother was doing there, and when it became apparent she had forgotten about him, he coughed and said, "Remember me? I want to know what your brother is doing here. How did he find us?"

Birds Landing tore herself from her sibling. "Forgive me. His name is Thunder Cloud. He was off hunting when Kutler and Tork came to our village, and when he learned what they had done, he came to Polson to find me. Since he dared not let himself be seen, he watched from a gully." Birds Landing spoke to Thunder Cloud and he replied. "He says that he saw Indian women going in and out of the Whiskey Mill, and guessed that is where I must be. He was nearby when you rescued me." She squeezed her brother's hand. "He followed, and only now caught up."

Fargo noticed how young Thunder Cloud was, and

the look of dislike the warrior gave him. "Have you told him you and I are friends?"

Birds Landing hesitated. "He knows what we did and he does not approve. But he never likes it when I am with a man, whether the man is white or red."

Just what Fargo needed. "What is he liable to do about it?" He was not fond of the idea of taking an arrow in the back.

After a brief, sharp exchange, Birds Landing said, "He will not do anything. He understands it is between you and me."

The way the warrior was looking at him, Fargo was not entirely convinced. "Has he seen any sign of Durn and his men?"

Another flurry resulted in: "He says we have lost them. That they gave up and turned back toward Polson."

That was good news in two respects. "Then we are safe," Fargo said in relief, "and I can leave you here with your brother and get on with what I came here to do."

"Leave me? So soon after—" Birds Landing caught herself. "Must you?" she asked simply.

"Yes." Fargo had learned a lot so far, about how Durn was taking over Polson. But one thing he had not learned, and which the army would want to know, was how Big Mike Durn intended to take over the entire territory.

"If you go back, Durn will have you killed."

"He is welcome to try," Fargo said, and began gathering up his saddle blanket and saddle.

"I am worried for you," Birds Landing said. "You are one and they are many."

"I'll be fine."

Fargo walked to the Ovaro. Were it not for the brother's glares, he might be inclined to stay the night. He threw on his saddle blanket and smoothed it out, then saddled up. Tying his bedroll and saddlebags on took no time at all. As he stepped into the stirrups,

Birds Landing came over and held out her hand to shake, white fashion.

"I better not kiss you. Thunder Cloud would not like it."

"He sure doesn't like me much," Fargo remarked.

"Do not take it personal," Birds Landing said. "If we had not made love, he would like you fine."

Fargo doubted it.

As if she had read his thoughts, Birds Landing said, "Then again, he is not all that fond of whites. He resents being forced to live on a reservation."

A lot of Indians resented it, with good cause, Fargo reflected. In too many instances, a tribe was marched hundreds of miles to their new home, which often was in a region with too little game and not enough water, areas the whites did not want for themselves. The Flatheads were lucky in that respect; the government was permitting them to stay on their own land.

"Make yourself scarce until Durn has been dealt with," Fargo advised. "He will not be riding roughshod over people much longer." Fargo touched her cheek, then gigged the Ovaro. He swore he could feel the brother's eyes bore into his back as the night engulfed him.

Fargo held the Ovaro to a walk. Once he was down out of the hills, he swung toward a trail that would take him into Polson from the south. All things considered, it seemed wise to ride in from a different direction.

The wilderness was alive with the cries of animals, predators and prey alike. None of the meat-eaters came anywhere near him, though, and he reached the trail without mishap.

Fargo was bone tired. He had been on the go all day without much rest. He intended to treat himself to a cozy bed and to treat the Ovaro to a stall in the stable. The prospect set him to grinning but his grin faded when a loud caterwauling fell on his ears. "It can't be," he said.

But it was.

Fargo went around the next turn, and there, staggering toward him while merrily singing off-key, was none other than Thaddeus Thompson, the ever-present bottle in hand.

Thaddeus took a swig, went to wipe his mouth with his sleeve, and took a step back. "You again!"

"Small world," Fargo said drily.

"What are you doing? Following me?"

"If I was, wouldn't I be behind you?"

Thaddeus looked over his shoulder, and chuckled. "When I am this booze blind, I can't tell front from back and sometimes up from down."

"How are things in Polson?" Fargo asked.

Slurring his words atrociously, Thaddeus said, "There was a ruckus earlier. I heard that one of Big Mike Durn's Indian girls got away, and he is none too happy."

"You don't say." Fargo feigned innocence.

"Yep. Somebody knocked two of Big Mike's toughs over their noggins and lit out with her." Thaddeus tittered. "It serves him right, the murdering bastard."

"Has Durn returned yet?"

"A couple of hours ago. Him and his men were plumb tuckered out, and he was growling at them fit to bite off their heads."

"Have you heard who took the Indian girl?"

"No one knows. Of if Durn does, he hasn't said." Thaddeus wet his throat again. "Sally Brook is right pleased, though. I heard her tell Durn that it was too bad all those girls didn't get away."

"How did Durn take that?"

"How do you think? He stomped into his saloon as mad as an old bull. Sally takes an awful chance mouthing off to him, but she is the only one who can get away with it."

Fargo looked forward to talking to her. "Want me to see you to your cabin, old-timer?"

Thaddeus snorted. "What the hell for? I'm not helpless."

"What about that griz—" Fargo began.

45

"Old One Ear? Don't start with him again. He is practically my pet."

The mention sparked Fargo to ask, "That reminds me. Have you heard anything about Mike Durn having a pet of his own?"

"Is it a polecat?" Thaddeus rejoined, and cackled.

"I take it that is a no."

"If he has one, no one has told me. Now be on your way. I have half a bottle yet to drink and the night ain't half over."

"Are you sure you can make it? You look fit to bounce off trees."

"How do you think I stay on my feet?" Beaming, Thaddeus fondled the bottle and walked on by. His off-key singing again rose to the stars.

Shaking his head, Fargo clucked to the Ovaro.

The lights of Polson were a mile off when hooves pounded and half a dozen riders swept across the trail, blocking it. Fargo drew rein, his elbow crooked so his fingers brushed his Colt. He did not recognize any of them except the small man in the middle.

Tork hefted his Sharps, then said, "Well, look who we have here. Mr. Durn was wondering what happened to you. Where have you been?"

"None of your damn business," Fargo said.

"Don't prod me, mister," Tork snapped. "We have about ridden our horses into the ground hunting for whoever took one of Mr. Durn's squaws. He is of the opinion it might be you."

"I better go have a talk with him. Where is he?"

"Back at the Whiskey Mill," Tork answered. "We will escort you in. But first, hand over your six-shooter."

"No."

Tork bristled with, "There are enough of us that you will be lucky to get off a shot."

"So long as the shot I get off is aimed at you," Fargo called the little man's bluff.

"You don't scare me none," Tork sneered. But he

did not make an issue of it. "Go on ahead of us and we will follow."

"I will do the following," Fargo told him. "Less chance of a bullet in the back that way."

"If you and me tangle, it will be head-on," Tork predicted. "I am no coward." He reined his mount around, bawling, "We will do as he wants, boys. He gets to go on breathing until Mr. Durn says different."

A hardcase on the right spat on the ground. "I don't much like how he tells us what to do."

"I am the one telling you," Tork said. "And I speak for Mr. Durn. Now spur that critter of yours or your neck will need a new head." So saying, he trained his Sharps on the malcontent.

Fargo half hoped they would shoot one another but the other man did not have the backbone to buck Tork, and fell in with the rest.

On the ride back Fargo had plenty of time to think over what he was going to say.

Polson had quieted. Fewer people were on the street and some of the houses were dark. He let Tork's bunch go in first. At the batwings he paused to check the lay of the saloon.

Big Mike Durn was at the bar. He was not alone. Seven of his men were drinking with him. Kutler was nowhere to be seen, but Grunge was there. About half the tables had card games going. Fewer maidens were mingling with the customers.

Fargo pushed on through.

Tork had reached the bar and said something to Durn, who turned with his elbows on the counter and regarded Fargo with his usual cold smile. The cardplayers paid little attention as Fargo wound among the tables and planted himself a good six feet from the ruler of the Polson roost. "What is this about me helping one of your girls get away?" he started right in.

"Mr. Fargo," Durn said with feigned politeness. "Perhaps you would be willing to account for your whereabouts tonight."

"I would not."

"Might I ask why?"

"I will tell you what I told your cur," Fargo said. "What I do is my own affair."

"I ask you to reconsider," Big Mike said.

"And if I don't?"

Durn snapped his fingers. Instantly, Tork and Grunge and the others turned with their rifles leveled or their revolvers out and pointed.

Fargo froze.

"If you don't," Durn said, still acting polite as could be, "I will snap my fingers again and my men will turn you into a sieve." His cold smile widened.

"It is your choice."

7

Fargo had a contrary streak in him a mile wide, and he showed it now. He clamped his jaw and said nothing.

Mike Durn arched an eyebrow. "I have heard of stubborn but you are ridiculous. Or is it something else?" His forehead knit in perplexity.

Fargo stayed silent.

"Whether you are or you aren't, you are damned clever," Durn paid him the same compliment Birds Landing had. "But I can be clever, too."

The others were grinning or smirking.

A sharp jab in the small of Fargo's back explained why.

"Remember me?" Kutler said. "Give me an excuse and I will bury my bowie all the way in."

Fargo inwardly swore. He had not kept an eye on what was going on behind him, and had paid for his mistake.

"I commend your timing," Durn said to his lieutenant.

"We came back for a change of mounts," Kutler said. "Ours were tuckered out."

"Any sign of her yet?"

"Not a trace. I sent men to her village but they won't be back until tomorrow afternoon."

"You have done well," Durn said. He walked up to Fargo. "Now then. What to do about you?"

"Let me blow his head off," Tork requested. "He doesn't use it much anyway."

Some of the men laughed.

Durn reached out and plucked the Colt from Fargo's holster. "I will hold on to this for a while. You don't mind, do you?"

More laughter, and Fargo grew warm with rising anger.

Kutler asked, "Want me to finish him here and now, Mr. Durn? Or take him outside and gut him so I don't make a mess of your floor."

"Neither," Durn said. "Not until I learn why he is here. If my suspicions are right, and we kill him, it will confirm *their* suspicions." Durn stepped back and gave the Colt to Tork. "Now then," he addressed Fargo. "I will ask you one last time. Did you have a hand in spiriting that squaw away tonight?"

Fargo did not respond.

"You are becoming tedious," Durn said. "Killing you is not the only choice I have. You would do well to consider that."

"Do what you have to," Fargo said.

Mike Durn cocked his head and scratched his chin. "You puzzle me. You truly do. I will get it out of you one way or another. You must know that."

"I know you love to hear yourself talk."

Durn sighed. "Why make it hard on yourself?" He waited, and when Fargo did not say anything, he sighed again. "Very well. We will play this out the way you want. Mr. Kutler, step back. Mr. Tork and a few of you others, push these tables and chairs out of the way."

The men were eager to comply.

Fargo suspected what was coming and focused on the man with the huge hands. He turned out to be right.

"Mr. Grunge, he is all yours."

Grunge unbuckled his gun belt and set it on the bar. Flexing and unflexing his thick fingers, he came over and regarded Fargo as he might a puppy he was about to kick. "How bad do you want me to hurt him, Mr. Durn?"

"Bad," was Durn's reply. "I want him in pain for a week."

"You heard him, mister," Grunge said, and balled those enormous fists of his.

Fargo did not care how big the man's hands were. So what if they could shatter doors? So long as he did not let them connect, he could hold his own. And he was considerably quicker than most.

"You don't seem scared."

"There is no one to be scared of."

"Insulting me isn't all that smart," Grunge said, and hit him.

The blow to Fargo's chest sent him tottering. He was more in shock than pain; he had not seen Grunge's fist move.

"That was a taste of what is in store for you. I have never been beaten in a fist fight. Not ever," Grunge stressed, and raised his hams with their walnut-sized knuckles.

Fargo raised his own fists. He had been in more than his share of bruising brawls and usually held his own. He told himself that Grunge had caught him by surprise, and it would not happen again.

Then Grunge closed, and thinking became a luxury Fargo could not afford. He was up against a human whirlwind.

Grunge rained blows: jabs, thrusts, uppercuts, overhands. He did not pause, did not stop to catch his breath, did not relent whatsoever. He punched and punched, each blow a blur.

Fargo was driven back under the onslaught. He blocked and ducked and weaved but as quick as he was, Grunge was his equal. For every three or four blows Fargo countered or evaded, one got through, and each that landed felt like a hammer.

The plain truth was, Fargo had never been hit so hard.

Durn's men were whooping and hollering, their brutal natures relishing the spectacle. Durn, oddly, was quiet.

Fargo did not give up hope. One punch was all it would take, a solid blow to Grunge's jaw and the fight would be over. As he circled, he was alert for an opening, and suddenly it came. Grunge unleashed a roundhouse right that missed. Before he could recover, Fargo slammed an uppercut to his chin, putting everything he had into it.

But all Grunge did was take a step back, and blink. "Is that the best you can do?"

Fury boiled in Fargo. Fury that he was being treated as if he were a no-account weakling. He threw a left jab as a feint and, when Grunge sidestepped, landed another blow to the chin. This time Grunge nearly went down.

Smiling grimly, Fargo said, "I can do better."

"For that," Grunge said, "I will stop going easy on you." He waded in, his arms driving like pistons in a steam engine.

Giant fists seemed to be everywhere. Fargo blocked as best he could and dodged as best he was able but blow after blow still scored, and each jarred him to his marrow.

Vaguely, Fargo was aware of the onlookers cheering Grunge on and calling for his blood. Not just Durn's men, but nearly everyone in the saloon. Cardplayers had interrupted their games to come and watch. Drinkers had put down their drinks and were adding their shouts and cheers to the uproar.

A glancing blow to the head sent Fargo reeling. He shook the effect off but he could tell his vitality was ebbing. He slipped a left jab, retreated from a right uppercut, and thought his ribs had caved in when Grunge caught him in the side. Doubled over, he backpedaled, and the next thing he knew, he bumped into the bar.

"Are you ready to tell Mr. Durn what he wants to know?" Grunge asked.

"Go to hell," Fargo hissed between clenched teeth.

Grunge glanced at Durn, who nodded and said, "Pound the stubborn fool into the floor."

Fargo's world became a haze of fists and pain. His body throbbed with agony. His arms were so heavy, he could barely lift them. His legs wobbled. He was being beaten and there was not a damn thing he could do. Or was there?

Punching with impunity, Grunge had waded in closer.

With an effort, Fargo concentrated on his opponent's chin. He absorbed more punishment, and then, for a few seconds, Grunge slowed. Fargo threw all he had into a right cross that he hoped would bring the man down. He was sure it landed, but a strange thing happened. Instead of Grunge buckling, Fargo felt his own legs start to give out.

A fist filled his vision, and there was blackness and muffled sounds, and then even the sounds faded.

Fargo's first sensation was of floating in a sea of pain. He hurt everywhere. From his hair to his toes, every inch of him was in torment. Gradually the pain lessened to where he became conscious that he *was* conscious, that he was lying on his back on something soft, and that, oddly, he could smell lilacs.

Fargo opened his eyes. The right one worked as it should but the left eye was swollen half shut. Above him spread a flowered canopy. He was in a four-poster bed in a nicely furnished bedroom. The pink walls and pink quilt hinted at the gender of the owner. He licked his lips and found the lower lip puffy.

Fargo raised his right arm. His hand had swelled and his knuckles were scraped raw. Someone had cleaned up the blood and applied ointment to each knuckle.

A blanket covered him to his chest. Fargo did not need to lift it to tell he was naked. He went to sit up but his ribs protested and his head began to throb so he eased back down. He summed up the state of affairs with a heartfelt, "Damn."

Not five seconds later the bedroom door opened and in swept a lovely blond vision with emerald green eyes and full strawberry lips, wearing a light green dress that swished with each stride of her long legs. "I thought I heard you say something. Good morning."

"I was out all night?"

"You have been unconscious for three days, Mr. Fargo. For a while it was nip and tuck, and I feared I would lose you." The blond vision had a radiant smile. "I am Sally Brook, by the way."

"I know," Fargo said. "Thaddeus Thompson told me about you."

"Ah," Sally said. "And Mike Durn told me a lot about you, but not why he had you beaten and thrown into the street."

"The street?" Fargo repeated.

Sally nodded. "That is where I found you. No one else would go near you, so great is their fear of Durn. I took it on myself to bring you home and nurse you back to health."

"I am obliged," Fargo said. Not many people would put themselves out for a stranger as she had done.

"My motive is not entirely charitable," Sally Brook said. "From what I gather, you are Mike Durn's enemy."

"After what he has done, it will be him or me," Fargo said.

"I am his enemy, too," Sally said, "in that I have been trying my utmost to stop his trafficking in Indian girls. They are brought to his place against their will and degraded in ways I can only describe as despicable." She caught herself. "What am I thinking? Enough about my crusade. You must be famished. I was only able to get a little food and water into you while you were out."

The mention caused Fargo's stomach to rumble. "I reckon I am starved," he admitted. "But there are things I need to know first."

"Such as?"

"For starters, my horse," Fargo said. "Did you see an Ovaro out front of the saloon?"

"I am afraid I do not know a lot about horses,"

Sally said. "But if by Ovaro you mean a black and white stallion, it was nuzzling you when I first saw you. I assumed it must be yours, and sure enough, Kutler came out of the Whiskey Mill and confirmed it."

"Did he say anything else?"

"Only that you were a fool to buck Mike Durn, and that I was a fool not to accept Durn's long-standing invitation to supper. All that while he helped me drape you over your saddle." Sally indicated a window to his left. "Your horse is out back. Don't worry. My yard is fenced so he can't wander off."

"More to be obliged for," Fargo said.

"Save your thanks. When you hear what I have in mind, you might not be so grateful."

"Care to give me a clue?"

"Let's just say that since we share a common enemy, we should work together for the common good." Sally Brook put a hand to his forehead. "Your fever is down. I will bring you hot soup directly."

"How about some coffee? Or better yet, a glass of whiskey."

"I run a millinery, not a saloon," Sally said, not unkindly. "But I might have an old bottle in one of the kitchen cabinets." She patted his shoulder and whisked on out.

Fargo settled back. He must have been born under a lucky star. If she had not come along when she did, he might still be lying out in the street, only he wouldn't be breathing.

Rage bubbled in him like lava in a volcano. Mike Durn had made a mistake in not finishing him off. Because now it was personal. No one did to him what Durn had done. *No one.* It wasn't just that his body took a savage beating. It wasn't strictly pride, either. It went deeper than that. It went to the core of his being.

Fargo had never been one to forgive and forget. When someone hurt him, he hurt back. When someone tried to kill him, he killed them. It went against his grain to be stomped into the floor and then go on with his life as if nothing had happened. Mike Durn had a reckoning coming. Kutler, Tork, Grunge—especially Grunge—must answer for carrying out Durn's wishes.

Fargo made a silent vow. He was going to tear Durn's little empire out from under him.

Drowsiness put an end to his musing. He dozed off, only to be immediately awakened by the bedroom door opening.

"Here you are," Sally said sweetly. She bore a wooden tray with a large china bowl filled to the brim. Several slices of buttered bread were neatly stacked next to the bowl. "I trust chicken soup will do?"

"Will it ever," Fargo said hungrily. Placing his hands flat on the bed, he pushed himself up and braced his back against the headboard.

Sally carefully settled the tray in his lap and handed him a spoon. "Is there anything else I can get you?"

"My rifle. It should be in my saddle scabbard." Fargo wanted it by his side, just in case.

"I'm sorry. When I stripped your horse, the scabbard was empty. Someone must have taken it."

"I will add that to the list," Fargo said.

"List?" Sally said.

Fargo avoided answering by spooning soup into his mouth. It was best she did not know. After all she had done for him, he did not want to upset her. But before he was done, Polson would run red with blood.

8

Fargo was up and around three days later but he was so sore and stiff that the best he could do was hobble about for short spells and then crawl back into bed to rest. He discovered that Sally lived in the back of a frame house. The front half she had converted into a millinery. She sold dresses and bonnets, along with things like hairbrushes and combs and hand mirrors, and even a selection of colored beads prized by Indian women. Her selection was modest compared to millineries in, say, Denver or St. Louis, but since she had the only lady's store for a thousand miles around, she had a devoted if small number of clients. Her living quarters consisted of the bedroom, a kitchen, a parlor, and a sewing room.

Fargo also found out that she was spending her nights on a cot in the sewing room. He objected, and suggested they switch and she take her bed back.

Sally would not hear of it. "You are under my care, and my guest, and I would be a poor nurse and a worse host if I put you in my sewing room. You will recover more quickly with a nice, comfortable bed to sleep in."

When Fargo still insisted it did not feel right, she put her hands on her shapely hips and her emerald eyes blazed.

"I will not hear of it and that is final. Besides, I have an ulterior motive. You are one of the few allies

I have in my fight to stop Big Mike Durn from ruining the lives of more maidens."

"What about the rest of the tribe?" Fargo asked.

"I beg your pardon?"

"It is not just the women. Durn is luring a lot of Indian men into his saloon, plying them with liquor, and putting them in debt to him." Fargo paused. "Then there is his loco notion of one day running the whole territory."

"He has made no secret of his ambition," Sally said. "It explains why he is always stirring everyone up against the idea of a reservation, and why he is doing all he can to cause trouble between the whites and the Flatheads and other tribes."

Insight hit Fargo with the force of a physical blow. "Durn wants an all-out war."

"That would be my guess, yes. If he can incite the Indians into going on the warpath, the government might decide a reservation is a bad idea."

"Then Durn can take all the Indian land for his own." Fargo marveled that he had not seen it sooner.

"With that much land, he will, in effect, run the territory, just as he has been claiming."

Fargo sat back. It all made perfect, horrifying sense. And Mike Durn did not care one whit that the loss of life on both sides would be frightfully high. "Why haven't you reported this?"

"To who, exactly? We have no marshal. We have no sheriff. The only person in Polson with any authority is, ironically, Durn himself."

"The army can take a hand when a civilian stirs up an uprising," Fargo pointed out.

"Do you realize how far the nearest fort is? It would take me weeks to get there. And all I have are suspicions. I have no proof. Without that, what good would the army be?"

"They would send someone to investigate," Fargo said. Which Colonel Travis had done on the strength of a few rumors. If she had gone, Travis would have sent a whole company.

"Maybe I should have," Sally begrudged him. "But I doubt I would have made it out of Mission Valley. Durn has me watched day and night. Were I to rent a wagon, he would find out and want to know where I was going." She shook her head. "No. I am fighting Durn as ably as I know how. Which is to do some stirring up of my own. A lot of people don't like the way he treats the Indians. Especially how he is turning innocent maidens into doves. I fight fire with fire in the hope that if enough people see him for what he is, his scheme will fail."

Fargo conceded that made sense.

"But even there Durn has outfoxed me," Sally brought up. "He has been bringing in a lot of men, vermin who do whatever he wants. By now there are almost as many of his people as there are those who were here before Durn came. And more of his kind show up every day."

Fargo saw where she was leading. It wouldn't be long before Durn had enough backers to virtually do as he pleased. The realization sobered him. There was no time for him to go to Colonel Travis, not when it might take the colonel weeks to prevail on Washington to act. The army's wheels of command turned exceedingly slowly. By the time soldiers were sent, Indians and whites could be slaughtering one another. All it would take was one massacre for the newspapers to whip their readers into a red-hating frenzy, with dire consequences for the Flatheads and others.

Fargo had to act, and act soon. But there was not much he could do, the condition he was in. Three more days went by. Days of frustration, and growing impatience. Fargo had Sally ask around to learn if Birds Landing had been caught; apparently, she had gotten away.

The next morning, Fargo was in the kitchen fixing coffee when the back door unexpectedly opened and in strolled Big Mike Durn. Fargo instinctively reached for his Colt and frowned when his hand brushed his empty holster. "This is a surprise."

"It shouldn't be," Mike Durn said. Leaving the door open, he walked to the table and pulled out a chair. "I have a vested interest in Miss Brook."

"Sally is in her store." Through the open door Fargo glimpsed Kutler, Tork, and Grunge.

"It is not her I came to talk to," Durn informed him. "It is you."

Fargo leaned against the counter and folded his arms. "Me?"

"Surely you did not think I was unaware you were here? I know everything that goes on in Polson. *Everything*," Durn stressed.

"It must be nice to be God."

"It is," Durn said with a smug grin. "I am a generous god, too. I permitted you to stay so you could recover and be fit to travel."

"Permitted?"

"No one does anything in Polson without my say-so," Durn bragged. "But enough about me. Now that you are on your feet, the time has come for you to move on."

"What if I don't want to go anywhere?" Fargo said.

"You do not have a choice. By tomorrow morning you will be gone. Say, by ten o'clock. One minute past ten, and if you are still here, well—" Durn did not finish the threat.

"You want me out of your hair," Fargo said.

"I want you away from Sally," Durn corrected him. "She can be a headache, but I have designs on the lady. The two of you living here doesn't sit well with me."

"Are you jealous?"

"What do I have to be jealous about?" Durn snapped. "If I thought for a second that you and her had—" Again he stopped, and indulged in a sinister smile.

"What about my Colt?"

"What about it? I gave it to one of my men. Hoyt is his name. He lost his fording a river a week ago."

"And my rifle?"

"The Henry? I took a fancy to that myself. It is up in my room."

"I want them back," Fargo told him.

"Is there no end to your pigheadedness?" Mike Durn leaned toward him. "You don't tell *me* what to do. I tell *you*. And I am not about to give you a gun that you might use against me. Count your blessings that you are getting out of Polson with your hide intact."

But was he? Fargo wondered. He would not put it past Durn to have him ambushed on the trail. "Anything else?" he asked when the would-be lord of the territory did not get up and go.

"You impressed me the other night in the saloon. I have never seen anyone take the punishment you did."

"Go to hell. You made it happen."

Durn ignored the comment. "I doubt anyone in my employ could endure half of what you did. You are tough. Damned tough. Which is why I am willing to let you stay in Polson provided you abide by two conditions."

Fargo was genuinely surprised. "Two seconds ago you wanted me out of here. Now I can stay?"

"The first condition is that you do not so much as speak to Sally Brook, ever. The second is that you come to work for me."

All Fargo could do was stare.

"I can use a man like you. In your own way you are as famous as Jim Bridger and Kit Carson. Imagine if word got around that the famous Skye Fargo was riding for me. It would bring people over to my side who otherwise wouldn't give me a second thought."

"You're serious?"

Durn made a teepee of his hands. "It is an either-or proposition. Either you leave, or you stay and work for me. And before you say no, bear in mind that I can make it well worth your while once I run the whole territory."

"Do you walk on water, too?"

Big Mike Durn laughed. "I don't need to. I'm not

out to claim men's souls. I just want everyone to think as I think, to see that there isn't room for us and the redskins. That we must drive the red scum out or exterminate them."

Fargo glanced out the back door. Kutler, Tork, and Grunge were watching and listening, ready to spring to Durn's aid if need be. "You must need spectacles. From where I stand, there is plenty of space for both."

Durn's features hardened. "So you are one of those, are you? A red-lover? You care more about those who kill your kind than about those who are killed."

"I have lived with Indians. They are not the rabid wolves you paint them to be."

"Oh, no?" Durn half rose but sat back down. "Tell that to all the whites that Indians have slaughtered."

"Whites have done their share." Fargo could recite a long list. Whole villages wiped out, every warrior, woman, and child. Blankets tainted with disease given free to grateful Indians who died in the most horrible agony.

"They brought it on themselves," Durn snapped. "I doubt there is a white man on the frontier who hasn't lost a family member or a friend to those stinking devils, or knows someone who has." His voice dropped to a growl. "I lost my own parents."

"What?"

"You heard me. My mother and father were killed by hostiles. They were part of a wagon train bound for Oregon Country and the train was attacked. My parents were last in line. The Indians were on them before anyone could do anything. After it was over, the wagon boss found what was left of them." Durn gazed out the window but he was not looking at Sally's yard; he was peering into his past. "I will never forget the day I heard the news, and I will never forgive those filthy heathens for what they did."

"Which tribe?" Fargo asked.

"Eh?"

"Which tribe did the hostiles belong to?"

"What difference does that make? One tribe is as

bad as the other. Or haven't you heard the expression that the only good Indian is a dead Indian?"

"Too many times," Fargo said. That Durn hated all Indians over an atrocity committed by a few was not unusual.

"I have been looking for a chance to pay them back," Durn went on, "and now I have it."

Fargo could only abide so much. "You damned jackass. The Flatheads are friendly. So are the Coeur d'Alenes. Neither had anything to do with your folks dying."

"They are red, aren't they?" Durn stood and crossed to the door. "Remember. You have until ten o'clock tomorrow morning. My men will be keeping an eye on this place so don't try anything." He gave a little wave and strolled out.

Fargo went to the door and watched. He heard footsteps behind him.

"I was out in the hall," Sally said. "I heard every word. I still cannot condone what is he doing, but now I understand why."

"Why here?" Fargo wondered out loud, turning.

"Excuse me?"

"Out of all the towns and settlements west of the Mississippi, what brought Durn here?"

"I can answer that. He told me once. Apparently he got into trouble over a killing and came west one step ahead of a lynch mob. He had heard about Flathead Lake and figured he could make a living here. He built a ferry, and the saloon, and was all set to start a new life. Then one day out on the street a Flathead bumped into him."

"On purpose?"

"No, no. The Flathead came out of the general store as Durn was walking past and they brushed shoulders. It was nothing, really. But Durn flew into a rage, and the next I knew, he started all this talk about driving the Indians out. It never made any sense until now." Sally clasped his hand. "But what about you? What will you do about tomorrow?"

"There is nothing I can do," Fargo said, thinking *for now*. "I will be gone by ten, like he wants."

"Oh." Sally's disappointment was transparent. "I am sorry to hear that."

Fargo closed the back door, clasped her elbow, and steered her to the other side of the kitchen, away from the window. "I am not really leaving, only pretending to. You can expect word from me through Thaddeus by the end of the week."

"I pray you are not biting off more than you can handle. You are one man and Durn has a small army."

"No one takes my guns from me and tells me to light a shuck," Fargo said. "No one."

"That is pride talking," Sally warned. "Unless you are careful, it can get you killed."

"Is there anyone else I can count on besides that old geezer and you?" Fargo needed to find out.

"Not that I can think of. A lot of people don't like what Durn is doing but they don't have the backbone to stand up to him." Sally paused. "That is too harsh. A handful would do more if they could but they have their families to think of. Durn is not above hurting their wives and children."

Fargo had bucked strong odds before, although rarely as lopsided as this. Big Mike held all the aces. But in life, as in poker, sometimes it was the joker in the deck that won the pot.

9

By nine thirty Fargo was saddled and ready to ride out. As he was pulling on the cinch he glanced over the Ovaro and spotted a man watching him from the corner of a nearby building. Leaving the Ovaro tied to the fence, he went into the kitchen for a last cup of coffee.

Sally Brook was puttering around trying not to be glum. She filled a china cup decorated with roses and set it on a saucer in front of him. "I am sorry it has to be like this."

"I keep telling you. It isn't over. It is just beginning."

"And I keep telling you that there are too many of them." Sally brushed at a lock of golden hair that had fallen over an eye. "It might be better if you really did leave. For your own sake, if nothing else."

"What about the Flatheads and the other tribes?" Fargo responded. "Or don't you care if they are driven from their land or wiped out?"

"You know better. But I also care about you—" Sally caught herself, and self-consciously smiled. "There. I have said it. I have grown a bit fond of you during your convalescence." She placed her hand on his shoulder. "I don't want anything to happen to you."

Fargo gripped her wrist, pulled her down, and kissed her on the mouth. She was so startled, she recoiled.

"What was that for?"

"I have grown fond of you, too," Fargo said. He particularly liked her full, ripe body. It was easy to see why Mike Durn fancied her.

"Oh." Sally coughed, then said, "You can let go of my arm now."

"Right after I do this," Fargo said, and rising, he kissed her again, fusing his mouth to hers. She stiffened, then gradually relaxed, her hands straying to his shoulders. When he pulled back, she had a new gleam in her lovely eyes.

"That was nice."

"It was supposed to be." Fargo glanced out the window to be sure no one had seen, and sat back down. "Once this is over, there are a lot more where that came from. If you are interested," he teased.

"Very much so," Sally said. "But I should warn you. I am not all that worldly. I have not been with a lot of men."

Fargo swallowed half the cup at a gulp. "You make it sound like that should matter."

"I am only saying I do not have a lot of experience," Sally clarified. "I wouldn't want you to be disappointed."

Fargo admired the swell of her bosom and the suggestion of willowy legs under her dress. "Don't worry there."

Sally gave a nervous little laugh. "Listen to me. I am becoming too brazen for my own good. Next I will be picking up men on street corners."

"I doubt that." Fargo glanced out the window again and there was the same man who had been spying on him earlier, in the next yard. He got up and drew the shade.

"Was the sun bothering you?" Sally asked.

"Something was," Fargo answered, and leaned against the table to finish his coffee.

"How will you get in touch with me if you need to?"

"I will find a way," Fargo assured her.

"But what if you are killed? How will I find out? Durn is not likely to come right out and tell me."

"I wouldn't put anything past him," Fargo said. He put down the cup and pulled his hat brim low. "Time to be going."

Sally stepped in front of him. "Be careful. Please."

Fargo kissed her a third time, a long, languid kiss with her flush against him so that her breasts were cushioned by his chest and he could feel the swell of her thighs against his legs. He started to stir where a man always stirred. Reluctantly, he went out, opened the gate, and forked leather. She stayed in the doorway, a portrait of sadness.

"I will be thinking of you."

Fargo would be thinking of her a lot, too. Without her clothes on. He gigged the Ovaro and rode around the house and on down Polson's dusty main street.

Big Mike Durn and half a dozen of his underlings, including Kutler, Tork, and Grunge, were waiting out front of the saloon. Durn saw him and came out into the street. "You are early," he said when Fargo drew rein.

"No sense in testing your good nature," Fargo remarked.

"No danger of that since I don't have one," Durn shot back.

Fargo lifted the reins to go on. "Until we meet again."

"This is the last time we will see one another," Durn informed him. "And I can't say it has come soon enough to suit me."

"You take an awful lot for granted."

Big Mike Durn did not take offense. Instead, he called out, "Hoyt!" From around the Whiskey Mill came a trio of tough characters on horseback.

"What is this?" Fargo asked.

"As if you didn't expect it," Durn said. "These three will make sure you leave Mission Valley. Try to turn back and they will bury you."

Fargo suspected they were under orders to plant

him anyway. He studied them from under his hat brim. His Colt was in the holster of the heaviest of the three. Hoyt, evidently.

"Any message for Sally when I see her tonight?" Durn rubbed it in. "On second thought, I don't want to hear your name mentioned ever again." He moved out of the way. "Off you go. Six months from now, when I am in control, you are welcome to come back and we will toast my good fortune."

"That will be the day." Fargo clucked to the Ovaro and pretended he did not notice Grunge rub his over-sized knuckles and grin, or hear Tork mutter something about people who did not live up to their reputations.

The morning was crisp and clear, the sky a vivid blue from horizon to horizon, with only a few puffs of cloud. A golden eagle soared high on the currents off the mountains, making for Flathead Lake.

Fargo rode south at a leisurely pace. It would not do to unduly tire the Ovaro, not with the hard riding that was to come later. Every now and again he glanced over his shoulder. Hoyt and the others stayed a couple of hundred yards back, close enough that they would not lose him if he tried to slip away. Little did they know what he had in mind.

Midway between Polson and the St. Ignatius Mission, Fargo reined to the east toward the foothills. His plan was to get the three men up into the hills and spring a nasty surprise, but he went only a short way when hooves pounded and they swept down on him on either side, Hoyt swinging ahead to block his path, then drawing rein.

"Where in hell do you think you are going, mister?"

"Is something the matter?" Fargo innocently asked.

"Don't take me for a fool," Hoyt rasped. "Mr. Durn said you are to leave this valley."

"What do you think I am doing?"

Hoyt leaned on his saddle horn, his other hand on Fargo's Colt. "I told you not to take me for a fool. I know all the trails in and out of here, and there isn't one in the direction you are heading."

"You don't say." Fargo looked all around as if he was confused. No one was in sight. He decided not to wait until they reached the hills.

"I thought you are supposed to be some sort of scout," Hoyt said. "How can you not know where you are heading?"

"This is my first time here," Fargo lied. Without being obvious, he slipped his boots free of the stirrups.

"If you ask me, you are next to worthless," Hoyt said, eliciting chuckles from his companions. He motioned to the south. "Keep going in that direction. I will holler when we get to the trail out of here."

"I am obliged," Fargo said. He lifted the reins as if he was about to ride on. They relaxed a trifle, thinking they had him buffaloed, and were unprepared when Fargo suddenly whipped around in the saddle and backhanded the man on his right across the face. Almost in the same instant he thrust his left leg up and out and caught the man on his left in the middle, nearly unhorsing him.

"Look out!" Hoyt squawked, and went for the Colt.

A jab of Fargo's spurs, and the Ovaro bounded forward. Fargo pole-armed Hoyt across the chest, then was in the clear. He bent low as a revolver cracked and a leaden bee buzzed his ear.

The valley floor was broken by stands of trees and patches of thick brush. Fargo raced for a cluster of spruce and pines. Another shot boomed but it, too, missed. Then he was in the stand and undoing his rope. He swept around a spruce, drew rein, and shook out the noose.

One of the cutthroats came galloping past. The second man was only a few yards behind.

That left Hoyt.

Fargo timed it perfectly. His arm rose and the noose licked out and over, settling as neatly as could be over Hoyt's head and shoulders. A lightning dally, and the deed was done.

Hoyt was catapulted backward off his horse and crashed brutally hard to the earth. He rolled after he hit and more of the rope wound around his arms, pinning them. His horse kept going.

Vaulting down, Fargo flipped Hoyt over. Hoyt's holster was empty. Keenly aware he did not have much time, Fargo scoured the grass, turning in circles. The Colt was nowhere to be seen.

"Frank! Sam!" Hoyt recovered enough to bellow. "He has me! Get back here!"

From off in the stand came shouts. The other two were on their way back.

In growing frustration Fargo bent low over the grass. The Colt had to be there somewhere. Hooves drummed, growing louder. He was about to get back on the Ovaro and get the hell out of there when sunlight gleamed off metal. He ran over. Just as his fingers wrapped around the Colt's smooth grips, the vegetation parted and out thundered the two hardcases.

A pistol roared, kicking dirt at Fargo's feet. Whirling, Fargo fired from the hip, fanning his Colt twice in swift cadence. The man on the right was punched backward as if by an invisible fist, and toppled.

The other one was taking aim. Fargo fanned another shot, coring the man's chest. It jolted him, but he stayed in the saddle and snapped off a reply as he swept on by.

Fargo spun, taking deliberate aim. But the rider was in the trees before he could shoot. He backpedaled toward the Ovaro. Suddenly something hooked him behind his ankles, and his legs were swept out from under him.

It was Hoyt's doing. He had sat up and was furiously struggling to shed the rope.

Fargo's shoulders absorbed the fall. In a twinkling he was up in a crouch, only to find the other rider bearing down on him. A slug missed him by a hand's width. He squeezed off one of his own.

The man jerked to the impact but stayed on. Another second, and he was past, and once again in among the trees.

Normally, Fargo kept five pills in the wheel. That meant he had one shot left. He needed to reload but he was denied the chance. Iron arms wrapped around his legs and he crashed down onto his hands and knees. He raked with the heel of his right boot and felt the spur dig into flesh. The vise around his legs loosened. Heaving upright, he was almost erect when a shoulder caught him in the midriff and he was violently bowled over.

The next moment, Fargo was on his back with Hoyt on his chest. He swung the Colt at Hoyt's temple but Hoyt grabbed his wrist and sought to tear the Colt from his grasp.

"Sam! I have him! Help me!"

Fargo heaved upward and Hoyt fell off his chest but clung to his arm. In desperation Fargo clubbed him with his other fist but Hoyt still would not let go. The crackle of underbrush warned Fargo that the other one was rushing to help. His back prickled in expectation of taking a slug.

Fargo rammed his left knee into Hoyt's gut, and at the same instant dropped his left hand to his ankle and the sheath that held his Arkansas toothpick. The hilt molded to his palm. The double-edged blade flashed once, twice, three times, and Hoyt deflated like a punctured waterskin.

A shot cracked.

But Fargo was already moving. He sidestepped, extended his arm, and planted his last shot smack in the center of the rider's forehead. It snapped the man's head back, and down he went.

In the quiet that descended, Fargo heard ringing in his ears. He began reloading. The shots would carry a long way; there was no telling who might show up.

Fargo wiped the toothpick clean on Hoyt's shirt and replaced the slender blade in the ankle sheath. He smoothed his pant leg, then went from body to body, turning out pockets. Between them he found over three hundred dollars, far more than he expected. Each of the three had at least a hundred, which caused

71

him to speculate it was money they had been paid—to kill him.

"Mike Durn is going to be mighty upset," Fargo said out loud, and wished he could see the look on Durn's face when word reached him.

Hoyt grunted. He was still alive, if barely. Coughing up blood, he rasped, "I hope to God he makes you suffer before you die."

"You won't be here to see it if he does," Fargo said, and shot him in the head. Gathering up the reins of the riderless horses, Fargo turned to climb on the Ovaro. He left the bodies where they lay. Coyotes and vultures had to eat, too.

Ready to head out, Fargo patted his Colt. *Now* let Durn try to ride roughshod over him. All he needed was his Henry and he would be whole again.

Suddenly the Ovaro whinnied.

Instantly alert, Fargo glanced in the direction the stallion was looking. A figure was hunkered in the shadows. Thinking it was another of Durn's wolf pack, Fargo cleared leather in a blur. But as quick as he was, he was not quick enough.

An arrow cleaved the air, seeking his throat.

10

Reflex took over. Fargo flung himself to one side and the arrow missed, but he swore he felt the fleeting brush of a feather. He raised the Colt to fire, only to have another figure rush out of nowhere and stand between him and the archer while frantically waving both arms.

"Do not shoot! It is us!"

To say Fargo was surprised was an understatement. "Birds Landing?" Anger coursed through him; she was supposed to be long gone. "What the hell are you doing here?"

The pretty young maiden came up and took his hand in hers. "You are not happy to see me?"

"No," Fargo bluntly responded. "It isn't safe for you anywhere in Mission Valley. Why did you come back?"

"I never left."

"But you told me you would," Fargo testily reminded her. "What if Durn gets his hands on you again?"

"I could not go," Birds Landing said quietly. "Not after you and I were—what is the word? Oh, yes. Intimate."

"Oh, hell," Fargo said.

"Please do not be mad. I started to go as I promised. But my heart would not let me." She smiled sweetly. "My brother and I have been watching Polson. We saw you leave, and saw the three men follow you. We followed them."

The mention of her brother reminded Fargo of the arrow that nearly transfixed his neck.

Just then Thunder Cloud came out of the shadows leading their horse. He had slung his bow over a shoulder.

"Why did he try to kill me?"

Birds Landing and her sibling exchanged a flurry of Salish. "He says that he thought you were going to shoot him. You did draw your revolver and point it at him."

"Are you sure he just doesn't want me dead?"

"Why would he want that?" Birds Landing rejoined. "He is not happy I laid with you but that is not enough of a reason for him to kill you."

"If you say so." Fargo was not entirely convinced.

Thunder Cloud said something and Birds Landing translated. "He says he is sorry."

"He is too quick on the bow string," Fargo groused.

"Oh, he is not sorry for that," Birds Landing said. "He is sorry that he did not take me away as you wanted."

Fargo realized he was still holding his Colt, and holstered it. "He should have tied you and thrown you over his horse."

"That is what a white man would do," Birds Landing said. "But the Salish never do violence to Salish."

Fargo was aware that some tribes severely punished any member who harmed another. "It was a mistake for you to stay. But we can remedy that. Climb on and get out of here."

"No."

"Damn it," Fargo fumed. "You know what Durn is capable of. Why are you being so stubborn?"

"I like you."

Fargo had no ready reply to that. Instead he said, "We can't stay here. Those shots might bring others. Follow me." He headed east, leading the other two horses.

Thunder Cloud, riding double with his sister, brought his sorrel up next to the Ovaro. He did not look pleased but Birds Landing was smiling.

"Please do not be mad. I cannot help how I feel about us."

Fargo refused to be pacified. For her own good he said gruffly, "There is no *us*. When I am done with Mike Durn, I will ride off and you will never see me again."

"I know that. But while you stay, I will not leave your side. My heart and your heart are like this." Birds Landing entwined her hands.

"Damn you, woman." This was the last thing Fargo needed.

"Whether you admit it or not, I speak with a straight tongue. I can feel how you feel in here." Birds Landing pressed a hand to her bosom.

Fargo smothered a string of oaths. He hated it when women made more out of making love than there was to make. Especially since he was not one of those men who lied to get women to part their legs. He never made empty promises, never professed love or the intention to marry them. But that did not stop females like Birds Landing from making a mountain of romance out of a bump of passion.

Thunder Cloud glanced over his shoulder at his sister and they broke into a heated argument. When they were done, Birds Landing laughed lightly.

"It might please you to know that my brother agrees with you. He wants me to go, too."

"You should listen," Fargo said, knowing full well she wouldn't.

"We can help you. We can spy on Durn and his men. Or follow them. Or whatever else you need."

"Can't you get it through that thick head of yours that Durn will kill you to make an example of you, if you are caught?"

Birds Landing shrugged. "We all die."

"What about your brother?" Fargo tried another tack. "Do you want him to die protecting you?"

75

"Nothing you say will change my mind. I always do as I think best whether others think it best or not."

This time Fargo did not hold it in. He swore, luridly.

Birds Landing laughed as if it were a great game to her. "The priest and the nuns would be shocked if they heard you talk like that. The priest says that swearing is a step on the stairwell to hell. His exact words."

Fargo regretted ever making love to her.

"You are quiet all of a sudden. Do not be upset. I am a grown woman. I can do as I please."

Fargo let out a sigh. For her sake, he would try one more time. "Just because a man and a woman make love doesn't mean they are *in* love."

"I know that."

"I do not love you, Birds Landing."

"You think you do not. But secretly you do."

An urge came over Fargo to grab her and shake her until her teeth rattled. Not that it would do any good. He rode moodily on until they had gone over a mile. A dry wash seemed as likely a spot as any to stop.

"My brother will hunt for us if you would like," Birds Landing offered. "I will make a meal."

"The only thing I want from you," Fargo said, "is to see you riding off."

"You do not mean that."

Fargo came close to doing something he rarely did—hitting a woman. A good smack or two might knock some sense into her. He wished he knew enough of her tongue to talk directly to her brother.

"So what now?" Birds Landing asked.

A question for which Fargo had no ready answer. "I need to think," he said, and walked off along the bottom of the wash. Before he came to the first bend he acquired a shadow at his elbow. "Go back."

"I would rather be with you," Birds Landing said. "You are troubled and I will soothe you."

Fargo wondered how she intended to do that, but he did not wonder long. No sooner were they around

76

the bend than she gripped his wrist and pulled him to her. Her warm lips sought his in hungry urgency. Under different circumstances Fargo would not have minded one bit. But if he responded, it would feed her misguided notion of being in love. He went to push her away when suddenly she cupped him, down low.

"See? You pretend you do not like me but I can feel you growing hard for me."

Fargo's own body was betraying him. "It's not that I don't like you—" he began, and knew he had made a mistake the instant the words were out of his mouth.

Beaming joyfully, Birds Landing covered his face with hot kisses. "I knew it!" she happily declared. "I will never leave you now."

The feel of her breasts, the taste of her tongue, were intoxicating. Struggling with his lust, Fargo pushed her back. He had to clear his throat to say, "When I say I like you, there is nothing more."

Birds Landing grinned. "Your body does not lie."

"Damn it." Fargo was appalled at how badly he had misjudged her. Usually he caught on when a woman was after more than a tumble in the grass. But she had fooled him completely.

"There must be something my brother and I can do to help you. You have but to name it."

"Why would he lend a hand?" Fargo asked. "He doesn't even like me."

"He will help because I am helping and he does not want any harm to come to me."

"At least someone in your family has some sense," Fargo remarked.

"Insult me all you want. You only do it because you care."

Fargo was at his wit's end. Nothing he said or did got through. Wheeling, he strode back. She quickly caught up, taking two steps for each of his.

"What is wrong?"

Fargo had had enough. He went to the Ovaro and opened a saddlebag. Inside was a coil of rawhide he used now and then for picketing the Ovaro to a picket pin, and for other odds and ends. Uncoiling it, he bent, drew his toothpick, and cut off a two-foot length.

Birds Landing watched with interest. "What is that for?"

"This." Suddenly grabbing her by the arms, Fargo spun her around and looped one end of the rawhide around her wrist. She divined what he was up to and tried to pull free before he could loop the rawhide around her other wrist but he was too fast for her.

"What do you think you are doing? Untie me this instant!"

A flick of Fargo's leg, and down she went. He caught her and lowered her onto her side. Pinning her legs with his, he tied her ankles. All done so slickly, she was bound and helpless before she could lift a finger to prevent it.

"You cannot do this!" Birds Landing protested.

Fargo slowly rose. Her brother had not intervened. Thunder Cloud was watching them, his expression hard to read. Fargo pointed at Birds Landing, then at Thunder Cloud's horse, and wriggled his fingers to simulate riding away.

"He will not do it," Birds Landing predicted, and launched into a long appeal to her brother in their own tongue.

Thunder Cloud's reaction surprised her as much as it surprised Fargo. He threw back his head and laughed. Then he came over, and white fashion, offered his hand to Fargo.

Fargo went him one better. After shaking, he took the reins to the two extra horses and placed them in Thunder Cloud's hands. The warrior looked at the horses, and then at Fargo, and something akin to warmth came into his eyes.

"Tell him they are his to keep for taking you away," Fargo said to Birds Landing.

"I will not."

Fargo shrugged. "I reckon he gets the idea anyway."

"Don't do this!" Birds Landing pleaded. "You need us. Durn is too formidable for you to fight alone. That is the word, yes? Formidable?"

"Save your breath." Fargo stepped to the Ovaro and gripped the saddle horn.

"Please!" Birds Landing begged.

Paying her no mind, Fargo was about to swing up when he remembered the two rifles in the saddle scabbards on the extra horses. He slid each out. One was a Sharps, the other a Spencer. A check of the saddlebags turned up ammunition for both. He gave the Sharps and its ammo to Thunder Cloud, who lit up like a candle.

"I am keeping this for myself," Fargo said, shaking the Spencer. At least until he reclaimed his Henry.

Thunder Cloud was caressing the Sharps as he might a lover. He indicated the horses and the Sharps and spoke a bit.

Fargo arched an eyebrow at Birds Landing.

"He says he misjudged you. He says you are a friend to the Salish, and to him."

Thunder Cloud added more.

Scowling, Birds Landing translated. "He says he will take me so far away, it will take me two moons to ride back."

Fargo chuckled. "Tell your brother I thank him."

Another argument ensued. Birds Landing sat up, her knees tucked to her chest, and glared at both of them. "The two people I care for the most, treating me like this."

"Be thankful I didn't spank you," Fargo said.

Birds Landing grinned in delight. "You still can if you want."

"Women," Fargo said. He swung onto the Ovaro, slid the Spencer into the scabbard, shoved the ammunition into a saddlebag, and was ready. He gave Birds Landing a last, fond look. "Try not to hate me. I did this for your own good."

"Hate you?" she repeated. "It shows you care, and it makes me care for you all the more."

Fargo nodded to her brother, and got out of there. He was glad to have Birds Landing out of his hair; she was one less problem. But now he faced a greater challenge. Mike Durn and his deadly pack of two-legged wolves must be dealt with. The key, as Fargo saw it, was Durn, himself. Should Durn be turned into worm food, the whole loco scheme to drive the Indians out would come to nothing.

Fargo made himself a promise. From that moment on, he would devote every waking moment to the extermination of Mike Durn. He would do whatever it took, and not let anyone stand in his way.

The bloodbath was about to commence.

11

Another wild night in Polson.

The Whiskey Mill was bursting at the seams. Piano music, loud voices, drunken singing, and an occasional angry curse testified to the liveliness within. The hitch rail was lined end to end.

Few people were on the street at that hour. The settlement's respectable citizens were in their homes and cabins, and many had already turned in.

Fargo approached in a wide loop that brought him up on the saloon from the rear. He drew rein well back from a square of light spilling from a window and dismounted. Removing his spurs, he slid them into his saddlebags, then shucked the Spencer and crept to the back door. It was not bolted. Nor did the hinges creak as he opened it a crack to peer inside.

A gloomy hall, lit by a small lantern hanging from a peg, was flanked by rows of narrow doors. Fargo warily opened the first one and discovered a small room barely wider than a closet and about eight feet long. A bed was the only furniture, a single blanket the only luxury. The next room was the same except that a tattered beaded dress hung on a hook on a wall.

These were the living quarters for the Indian girls. Windowless, dingy, with no heat or water, they reminded him of a dog kennel he visited once.

Fargo tried a door on the other side. It was pitch black within. He blinked when cold air struck his face. A dank scent tingled his nose, hinting at bare earth.

Wooden steps led down into virtual ink. He started to close the door, then stiffened.

From below came a sound that was not human, a low, long, eerie cry part growl and partly a keen of lament. Fargo had never heard anything quite like it. He listened until it faded, then quickly shut the door and moved on. He did not open any more doors until he was almost to the end. The door he chose was not plain pine, like the rest, but solid oak.

A luxurious bedroom lit by a large lamp spread before him. A broad bed, a mahogany dresser, a teak table and chairs, even a thick carpet, suggested that Fargo had found what he was looking for. Slipping inside, he shut the door behind him.

Fargo checked around the bed and under the bed. He noticed a closet and opened it. Neatly hung store-bought jackets and shirts and pants hung from a rod. Above, on a shelf, was a spare hat. Propped in a corner was the reason Fargo came. He smiled as he reclaimed the Henry and held it up so the lamplight gleamed on the brass receiver.

A sudden commotion in the hall caused Fargo to toss the Spencer onto the bed, whirl, and dart over near the door. He put his hand on the Colt and stared at the latch. It didn't move. He could hear voices, a lot of them, and footsteps, moving toward the back of the building. One voice rose above the rest, bellowing, "Hold her tight, damn you! I have lost one this week. I will not lose another."

Big Mike Durn.

Fargo waited until silence once again reigned. Carefully peeking out, he confirmed the hall was empty. But now light came from an open door toward the rear. The door, as he recollected, that led down to whatever lay below the saloon. Levering a round into the Henry, Fargo hurried toward it.

Light from a lantern revealed that the stairs wound in a spiral. Every nerve tingling, Fargo crept down them. The scent of cigar and pipe smoke hung in the air. So did the pungent odor of liquor. Laughter and voices came from somewhere below.

The stairs brought him to a dirt tunnel. Four feet wide and six feet high, it was a fairly recent excavation, if Fargo was any judge. At the far end was a door.

Bending so he did not bump his head, Fargo cautiously advanced. He was taking a gamble but he wanted to see what Durn was up to. A recessed door appeared on the right. He was surprised to find it was made entirely of iron. There was a small barred grille two-thirds of the way up and a thin slit no more than a few inches high at the bottom. He opened the slit and saw that it was wide enough to slide a plate or a bowl through. Putting his nose to the grille, he sniffed. An abominable reek assailed him, the stink of urine and feces and rotting flesh. He turned away before he gagged.

The hubbub at the far end had grown louder.

Fargo went faster. He needed to skedaddle before he was caught. But first he had to see. The door at the end, like the other, was metal. It did not have a vent at the bottom but it did have an opening near the top. Peering through, Fargo beheld a broad circular chamber dug out of the earth. In the center was a pit about ten feet in circumference. He could not tell how deep it was because his view was blocked by some of the more than two dozen people who ringed it. He was mildly surprised to see several white women among them.

Big Mike Durn was on the other side of the pit. On his right were Kutler, Tork, and Grunge. On his left, securely held by two more of Durn's pack, was a young Blackfoot woman in a tight red dress. She was struggling mightily but could not break free. Her hair was disheveled, and blood trickled from a corner of her mouth.

A few in the crowd were staring at her but most were gazing intently into the pit. One man pointed and said loud enough for Fargo to hear, "I sure as hell wouldn't want to be down there with that thing!"

An ominous growl filled the chamber. It hushed almost everyone, and those still talking stopped when Mike Durn held up a hand for silence.

A louder growl caused many on the rim to fidget with unease.

"What we have here," Durn declared, indicating the young woman, "is a horse that won't be broke. And what do you do when a horse won't let you ride it and tries to cave in your skull every time you try?"

Someone shouted, "You shoot it!"

"A horse, yes," Durn said with a grin. "But why waste lead on a squaw when there is a better way?"

Coarse mirth greeted his remark.

"This squaw's father is in debt to me. Out of the goodness of my heart I allowed him close to four hundred dollars in credit and he lost it all. He couldn't pay me back so I agreed his daughter could come work for me for a year to work off the money he owes. And what does she do?" Durn poked the young woman, hard, in the chest. "She refuses to do what I tell her. She puts on airs and won't let anyone touch her."

Murmuring broke out, but none of it, Fargo noted, was sympathy for the Blackfoot.

Mike Durn loved to hear himself talk. He had gone on with barely a break in breath. "But I was patient with her, as I am with all the red gnats. I gave her chance after chance to change her ways. Granted, I had to have her beat a few times, but not so she was crippled."

"You are a saint!" a man hollered, to the loudest laughter yet.

"That I am," Durn agreed, bobbing his chin. "I gave this bitch a roof over head and a bed to sleep in. I even gave her a new dress. And how does she repay my generosity? Last night she tried to scratch out the eyes of a man who put his hand on her behind. Can

84

you believe it? And then she had the gall to try and run away."

A hiss from the pit interrupted his speech.

"It is plain to me that there is no breaking her," Durn told his listeners. "I could send her back to her father. But she is bound to go around telling tales about how poorly she was treated, and stir up her tribe, and we can't have that." He adopted a sad expression. "I am afraid she leaves me no choice. She must share the fate of the other squaws who refused to do as they were told."

All eyes were now on the pit.

"I will tell her father that she did not like the work so I let her go. When they find her remains, they will blame it on old One Ear, as they did the others." Durn gazed down, and smiled. "No one suspects the truth. No one ever will."

A loud snarl brought a low cry from the young Blackfoot. She struggled harder, to no avail.

Fargo did not know for sure what was in the pit but he had some idea. The growls were a giveaway. Bears did not growl like wolves and wolves did not growl like mountains lions. If he was right, Durn had a hideous end in store for the young woman.

By intervening, Fargo would give himself away and possibly lose his own life. But he could not stand there and let it happen. And, too, here was a golden opportunity to put a permanent end to Mike Durn's ruthless spree.

Taking a step back, Fargo wedged the Henry's stock to his shoulder and sighted down the barrel, fixing a bead on Durn through the opening in the top of the door. He centered the sights smack between Durn's eyes. Then, holding his breath to steady his aim, he lightly curled his finger around the trigger. All it would take was a slight squeeze and Durn was done for.

"What the hell do you think you are you doing?"

A hand fell on Fargo's shoulder and he was spun

around. It was one of Durn's men, a beanpole with an Adam's apple a buzzard would envy. He wore a revolver and a knife and an amazed look.

"You! But you are supposed to be dead!" the man exclaimed, swooping his hand to his six-gun.

"You first," Fargo said, and shot him in the head. Instantly, Fargo turned back to the door but the harm had been done. Kutler and Grunge were between Durn and the door. He no longer had a clear shot.

Kutler cupped a hand to his mouth. "What is going on out there? What was that shot for?"

Many of the others had turned but no one was anxious to open the door. The few who could see through the opening could not see enough of Fargo to recognize him.

"Someone have a look out there!" Mike Durn commanded.

Fargo fired. He was aiming at Kutler. By downing him, he would have a shot at Durn. But at the very instant he squeezed the trigger, Grunge stepped in front of Kutler. The slug meant to core Kutler's forehead instead caught the man with the huge hands in the temple.

Grunge took one wobbly step and pitched over the rim.

All hell broke loose.

Men swore. Women screamed. Durn roared orders, and Kutler and Tork started around the pit.

Fargo began to turn as the face of another of Durn's cutthroats appeared in the opening.

"It's Fargo!" the man screeched. "I can see him as plain as day."

"Not any more," Fargo said, and shot him in the eye. Pivoting on a heel, he ran. He hoped that last shot would hold them back but he had not taken four strides when the door clanged open.

"Shoot him!"

"Kill the son of a bitch!"

A revolver boomed.

Spinning on the fly, Fargo banged off two swift shots

at a knot of men in the doorway. One went down. The rest scattered right and left, buying Fargo precious seconds. Pumping his legs, he flew along the tunnel.

"Damn your hides, *stop him*!"

That last was Big Mike Durn, and his rage practically shook the walls. Fargo kept one eye behind him as he covered the last sixty feet, and it proved well he did. A rifle barrel poked out. He dived, throwing himself flat as the rifle went off. Rolling onto his back, he answered and heard a yelp.

Fargo ran on. As he flew past the iron door with the grille and the slit, the foul reek filled his nose. It stirred a memory of a winter's day long past. He had been high in the Rockies, climbing toward a pass that would take him over a remote range, when he came on tracks in the light snow. Because he so rarely saw tracks made by that particular animal, he followed them a short distance, and wound up stumbling on the creature's lair. The stink that came from that lair was the same as the stink that came from the grille in the iron door.

Another shot warned Fargo this was not the time or place to recollect. He twisted and fired from the hip and the cutthroat at the other end flung up his arms and crumbled.

Fargo reached the spiral stairs. He climbed rapidly, his boots clomping noisily, but it could not be helped. He was almost to the top when the hallway above was filled with shouts of alarm.

More of Durn's men were rushing from the saloon.

Fargo did not slow down. He hurtled into the hall, palming and cocking the Colt as he emerged. Four men were charging toward him. Only one had a revolver out and went to shoot. Fargo was quicker. The rest decided the floor was the place to be.

The back door buckled to Fargo's shoulder. After the stuffy confines of the tunnel and the stairs, the cool night air was invigorating. He raced to the Ovaro, shoved the Henry into the saddle scabbard, and forked leather. A jab of his heels and he was away.

Fargo circled to the north toward Flathead Lake. Durn would expect him to head south to the main trail. But Durn was unaware he intended to stay until Durn was worm food.

Men came spilling out of the rear of the saloon. Pistols and a few rifles glinted in the starlight. They looked every which way but by then Fargo had blended into the darkness and was impossible to spot.

Big Mike Durn was conspicuous by his bellows. Everyone was to get their horse and join the hunt. He would lead one party, Kutler another, Tork a third. They were to spread out and head south.

"Five hundred dollars to the one who brings me Fargo's head!" Durn gave them extra incentive.

"Do you mean his body with his head still on?" a man asked.

"I mean his damn head!" Durn roared. "And if you cut it off while he is still breathing, you get another hundred!"

Fargo grinned. With all of them searching to the south, his head was safe for the time being.

But no sooner did the thought cross his mind than a horse and rider materialized in front of him and a gun hammer clicked.

"Hold it right there, mister, or be blown to kingdom come."

12

Fargo drew rein. It was so dark he could not see the man clearly, which meant the rider could not possibly tell who he was. "What are you up to, mister? If you are out to rob me, I do not have enough money to make it worth your while."

"I work for Big Mike Durn," the man revealed. "I am coming from the ferry."

Fargo had forgotten about Durn's ferry operation. The reminder gave him an idea.

"What is all that ruckus yonder?" the man asked. "Did you have anything to do with it?"

"I am headed for the ferry, myself," Fargo said. "I want to take it to the north side of the lake tomorrow."

"You didn't answer me about the ruckus."

"There was some shooting a bit ago," Fargo said. "Maybe it was a drunk on a spree."

The rider gigged his mount closer. "Turn your horse around. We will go find out."

"Unless you are the law, you have no right to make me." Fargo slid his near leg out of the stirrup.

"This is all the law I need." The man held up the revolver. "Now do as you are told. Nice and slow, if you know what is good for you."

Fargo started to rein around. Making it a point to keep his hands where the man could see them, he smiled and said, "Sheath your horns. I have nothing to hide. It is an inconvenience but I will go." His leg was rising on "will." He kicked the man on the hip, almost unseating him.

Squawking, the rider grabbed for his saddle horn.

Streaking his Colt up and out, Fargo slammed the barrel against the man's temple. A second blow sent him tumbling, unconscious.

The horse bolted toward Polson.

Fargo got out of there. He found a trail leading toward the lake and followed it at a trot. In less than a hundred yards he came within sight of the shore. At the edge of the trees he reined up.

The ferry resembled those that plied the mighty Mississippi. Constructed of large logs, it had a rail to keep passengers and stock from taking unintended dips in Flathead Lake. Heavy ropes moored the near end to a broad dock.

That much Fargo expected. What he did not anticipate were the two men hunkered over a small fire, drinking coffee. Their horses were picketed close by. Plastering another smile on his face, he gigged the Ovaro toward them, acting as casual as he could. "How do you do. Would you be the ferry operators?"

The men stood. The tallest took a step, his hand on his six-shooter, and replied, "We are the guards. What do you want?"

"What time does the ferry leave in the morning?" Fargo asked. "I want to be on it."

"Eight o'clock."

"That late?" Fargo pretended to be disappointed. Dismounting, he remarked, "I was hoping it would be earlier."

"We do not set the time, mister. Big Mike Durn does. If you have a complaint, take it up with him."

"Any chance I can have some of your coffee?" Fargo stepped close to the fire and held out his hands as if to warm them.

"If you have your own cup."

"In my saddlebags." Fargo brought his tin cup over and let the man fill it. He took a sip, and grinned. "This would do to float horseshoes. Just how I like it."

The man motioned toward the lights of Polson. "We thought we heard a commotion a while ago, and our pard rode off to see what it was about. You didn't happen to see him on your way here, did you?"

"I sure didn't," Fargo said.

"But he was on the same trail," the second man said. "You had to have seen him."

"I was off in the woods," Fargo said offhandedly, turning so he could watch them from under his hat brim. Neither had a hand on his pistol.

"That wasn't very smart. There is a bear on the loose, in case you didn't know, and hostiles to reckon with."

"I have seen the bear and he ran off."

"You were lucky. They say old One Ear has eaten more folks than all the other grizzlies in the mountains combined."

"He did not eat me." Fargo finished the cup and held it out. "Mind if I have a refill?"

"Help yourself," the first guard said, but he did not sound happy about sharing. "Just remember. Coffee doesn't grow on trees. It costs money."

Fargo bent and lifted the pot. It was over half full, heavy enough for his purpose. "Do you want me to pay you?"

"We will let you have one more. But any after that will cost you fifty cents a cup."

"That is more than I would pay in a restaurant." Fargo tilted the pot as if he were going to pour, then spun and slammed it against the man's head. Coffee spewed from the spout and the lid flew off, but the man folded like soggy paper.

The second guard clumsily went for his hardware.

Spinning, Fargo dashed hot coffee in his face. The man yelped and swiped a sleeve at his eyes. A swift blow to the chin brought him to his knees. Another to the head felled him, and left the coffeepot bent and empty.

Fargo tossed the bent pot to one side. Using a rope lying on the dock, he bound them, hands and feet. He gagged them, too, using one guard's bandanna and the other's sock.

The ferry was swaying slightly to the rocking motion of wavelets rolling off the lake. Big enough to transport several heavy wagons, it must have taken months to build.

Fargo grinned as he imagined how mad Big Mike Durn was going to be. In ten minutes he had gathered enough dead branches and dry grass. He spent another five spreading them over the ferry. Finally he walked to the fire, selected a burning brand, and came back.

"For your owner being a bastard," Fargo said to the ferry, and cast the brand onto the kindling.

The grass caught right away. Tiny flames sprouted and rapidly spread, growing larger. Several branches combusted and the flames leaped higher. The heat became intense.

Fargo backed away as the crackling and hissing rose. The blaze would be visible for miles. It might consume the dock, too. Nodding in satisfaction, he walked toward the Ovaro, stopping when he saw that one of the guards had revived and was glaring at him. Going over, Fargo bent and pulled the dirty sock out of his mouth.

"You miserable son of a bitch!" the man declared. "Why did you go and do that?"

"I want you to give Durn a message."

"That ferry was his pride and joy," the man said. "He will have your heart cut out while it is still beating."

"Tell him this is just the start."

"Didn't you hear me? Do you have any idea who you are up against? You are asking to be planted."

"Tell him it will get worse," Fargo said. "Let those who ride for him know they should get out while they can."

"Big talk, mister. After we bury you, we will have a good laugh."

"Try laughing with this in your mouth," Fargo said,

and punched him in the gut. The man doubled over, gasping and wheezing, his mouth open wide enough for Fargo to jam the sock back in. In retaliation the man tried to bite his fingers but Fargo jerked them back.

"Nice try."

The man's eyes were pools of hate.

Patting him on the head, Fargo said, "Remember my message to Durn. He should show up before too long."

By now the ferry was ablaze. Flames five and six feet high shot toward the sky.

Swinging onto the Ovaro, Fargo rode northwest, hugging the shore. He went about seventy-five yards, to a cluster of boulders, and again drew rein. Dismounting, he yanked the Henry from the scabbard and jacked a cartridge into the chamber. He took a seat on a boulder with his back to another and placed the rifle across his lap.

Now all Fargo could do was wait. The fickle whim of fate had thwarted him at the pit under the saloon; he would not let it thwart him a second time.

The ferry was an inferno. Its glow lit up the lake and the shore for a hundred feet in all directions. The two ferry guards were watching it burn while tugging at their bonds.

A grunt off in the undergrowth caused Fargo to stiffen. It sounded like a bear. But it was not repeated, and after a couple of minutes of silence he relaxed, convinced that whatever made the sound was gone.

Other noises came out of the night, the drum of approaching riders. Fargo raised the Henry but he was disappointed to discover it was Kutler's bunch, not Durn's. In a flurry of excitement they reined up. Kutler drew his bowie and proceeded to cut the guards loose. As soon as the gags were out of their mouths they chattered like chipmunks, and whatever they told Kutler made him mad.

Presently, a second group of riders arrived. Again,

Fargo raised the Henry. Again, he was disappointed. It was Tork and his party. Tork and Kutler conferred, and Tork looked even madder than Kutler.

Fargo could have shot either one. They were standing close to the dock and were easy targets. But if Fargo shot them, it would forewarn Durn, and Durn was the key.

The minutes became snails, creeping by one after the other. Just when Fargo was convinced Durn would not show up, more hoofbeats proved him wrong.

Big Mike was off his horse before it came to a stop. He ran to the dock and shook his fist in impotent fury. Kutler said something, then took Durn over to the guard Fargo had given the message to.

The moment had come. Fargo brought up the Henry and aligned the sights. All it would take was a shot to the brain or the heart. He opted for the head.

Fargo rarely shot anyone from ambush but desperate stakes called for desperate measures. Still, he hesitated. As far as he knew, Durn was unarmed, and Fargo had never shot an unarmed man in his life. He thought of Birds Landing, and the pit, and the creature Durn fed the women to—and he stroked the trigger.

Some people, it was said, lived under a lucky star. If that was true, then Mike Durn lived under the luckiest, for at the exact instant Fargo fired, Durn, in a fit of fury, whirled and struck the ferry guard.

The shot missed.

Fargo worked the Henry's lever but Mike Durn and his men were scattering like a bevy of spooked quail. Fargo hastily fired at Durn and thought he saw Durn wince. Another moment, and Durn was beyond the circle of light.

Fargo swore.

Some of Durn's men had dropped flat instead of running off. They were roosting pigeons, but it was not them Fargo wanted. He ejected the spent cartridge and inserted another. If only Durn would step back into the light—that was all Fargo asked.

Suddenly a rifle boomed uncommonly loud and lead

buzzed within a foot of Fargo's head. From the sound, it had been Tork's Sharps.

Fargo figured the little man had seen the Henry's muzzle flash. He rose to change position but had gone only a step when Tork shouted words he did not quite catch. But he could guess what it was. He dashed around the boulders a heartbeat before fireflies sparkled and a swarm of lethal hornets blistered the air.

To stay in those boulders invited a dirt nap.

Shoving the Henry into the saddle scabbard, Fargo vaulted up. More shouts warned him that Durn's cutthroats were converging. A flick of his reins and he melted into the darkness before they could spot him.

Fargo paralleled the lake. Now and then he had to thread through vegetation that grew clear down to the water's edge. He was in no hurry. He figured Durn would wait until first light to come after him.

He figured wrong.

The clink of a horseshoe on rock was Fargo's first inkling he was being chased. He glanced back, and there, at the limit of his vision, vague shapes hove out of the gloom. Seven or eight, by his count, coming on swiftly. He gave the Ovaro its head. No sooner did it break into a gallop than shouts arose.

"Do you hear that? It's him!"

"After him, boys!"

"Remember, we get paid extra for the bastard's head!"

Fargo did not like riding flat out at night. A hole, a rut, a fallen limb, a jagged rock could bring the Ovaro down with a broken leg, or worse. Hoping for the best, he goaded it to go faster. On his right, the shimmering surface of Flathead Lake flew past; on the left, darkling woodland. Suddenly a boulder the size of a cabin reared out of nowhere and he reined sharply to go around.

A rifle thundered and lead ricocheted off the boulder.

Tork and his Sharps again.

Fargo raced on. He reined toward the water where going would be easier, only to find a legion of boulders strewn about like so many giant marbles. He had no choice but to rein back toward the timber.

"I see him! There!"

"Faster, boys!" Tork bawled. "By God, we have him!"

Fargo glanced back. They were optimistic; they had not gained any ground. He faced front again.

Too late, he saw the low limb.

A tremendous blow to the chest ripped Fargo from the saddle and sent him tumbling.

13

Stunned and flooded with pain, Fargo was vaguely aware the Ovaro had not stopped. A tide of inner blackness threatened to wash over him but he resisted. Dimly, he was conscious of pounding hooves and loud voices, and he braced for certain discovery.

Thunder filled his ears. Riders were on either side of him. He tried to move his right hand to draw his Colt but his body would not do what he wanted.

Someone—it sounded like Tork—shouted, "There's his horse!" A fresh flurry of shots spiked Fargo with fear for the Ovaro's life. The pounding faded and quiet descended, complete, utter quiet.

Fargo's senses returned. He hurt. He hurt like hell. He tested his arms and poked at his chest and he decided nothing was broken. Sitting up, he listened but heard only the sigh of the wind.

Fargo got his hand under him, and stood. The same whimsical fate that had twice thwarted his attempts to put an end to Mike Durn had now saved his life. Thanks to the moonless night, Tork and his men had not seen him when he was lying practically under the hooves of their horses. It was a wonder none of their mounts had stepped on him.

Fargo started north, walking slowly at first and then faster as he regained his strength. He could not shake the awful feeling that he would find the Ovaro dead. But if that were the case, Tork and the others would have turned back by now, and there was no sign of them.

Striding purposefully along, Fargo was pondering his next move when a grunt similar to the one he had heard earlier brought him up short. Whatever made it was close, very close.

Anxious to go on, Fargo strained to pierce the gloom. Loud sniffing caused the nape of his neck to prickle. The thing was no more than twenty feet away, to his left. A rumbling growl told him it had caught his scent.

It was definitely a bear. Whether it was One Ear or another, Fargo had no way of knowing. He drew his Colt but he did not use it. A wild shot in the dark would only succeed in wounding the thing, and a wounded bear was ferocity incarnate.

Suddenly a huge bulk reared. The brute had risen on its rear legs and was sniffing again.

Fargo braced for the worst. If the bear attacked, he was done for. He would fight but he did not stand a chance against the steely sinews, saber teeth, and thick claws of one of the most formidable creatures on the continent.

Yet more sniffing.

Fargo prayed the bear had fed recently and would soon wander off. Each second he stood there was an eternity of suspense. He broke out in a cold sweat, and his mouth went dry.

The bear dropped onto all fours.

Fargo started to hike his leg to palm the Arkansas toothpick. He would stab at the bear's eyes and the throat, and maybe, just maybe, hurt it so badly he would drive it off. Buffalo could fly, too.

Another grunt, and just like that the great beast vanished. When a bear wanted, it could move as silently as a ghost, and this one slipped away with nary a sound to mark its passage.

Fargo stayed where he was. Sometimes bears circled to come at prey from behind. He scanned the woods but the nocturnal behemoth did not show itself. At last, convinced it was safe, he moved on.

Continuing to stay close to the lake, Fargo hiked for over a mile. The night around him came alive with the cries of wildlife; the howls of wolves, the yips of coyotes, the occasional screech of a mountain lion, and once, the roar of a bear that might be One Ear. Now and again the death squeal of prey spoke of a predator's success.

Fargo's brow puckered when he spied a triangle of red and orange ahead. Apparently Tork had made camp for the night. He crept along the water's edge until he saw figures seated around a fire and a string of tethered horses. They had pitched camp on an open strip of shore.

Fargo snuck as near as he dared. He removed his boots, drew his Colt and the toothpick, and holding them above the water, waded into the lake, moving slowly so as not to splash. The cold brought goose bumps to his flesh. The water rose to his knees, then to his waist.

Fargo figured Tork and his friends would not pay much attention to the lake.

Danger, if it came at them, would come from the woods. When the water was as high as his chest, he slowly moved toward them until he could hear what they were saying.

"—happened to him. He must have jumped off his horse when he saw he couldn't get away." This from a mustachioed man in a brown hat.

"Jumped, hell!" Tork snapped. He was poking at the fire with a stick. "That doesn't make any damn sense. A man like him, he would never let us catch his horse."

Fargo glanced at the string. Sure enough, the Ovaro was one of them, tied in the middle.

"You almost sound like you admire him," another man said.

Tork glared until the speaker averted his gaze, then snarled, "The only thing I admire is toughness. Durn is tough, and I respect him for that. Kutler is tough, and I respect him. I don't respect you because you

99

are a puny peckerwood who would not last a week in the wild by your lonesome." He jabbed the fire again. "Skye Fargo is as tough as they come. He has to be, the things they say he has done."

"No one can accuse him of being yellow," commented another. "He took on all of us to try and save that girl."

"He has done a hell of a lot more," Tork said. "He has killed Grunge and probably Hoyt, and those other two. And now he has burned the ferry. You realize what that means, don't you?"

The rest exchanged puzzled looks.

"Idiots," Tork spat. "He has declared war on us. He intends to tear down everything Durn has built up, and to wipe out all of us who ride for him."

"Single-handed?" a man scoffed.

"There are near twenty of us and only one of him," commented another. "He is the idiot, not us."

"Tell that to Grunge and Hoyt," Tork said.

"He is on foot now," yet another man remarked. "We will find him easy once the sun is up."

Tork snorted in disgust. "I am surrounded by jackasses."

The man with the brown hat said, "I still can't believe he had the sand to sneak into Big Mike's room and take his rifle back."

"There is the proof in the pudding," Tork said. "You wouldn't do it, and I might not do it, but Fargo did."

"What does that prove except that he has no brains?" asked someone else.

"It is a wonder you can piss without peeing all over yourself," Tork told him. "Let me make it plain. All of you are rabbits and Fargo is a wolf. And you know what wolves do to rabbits."

"I am not afraid of him," the same man blustered.

"Which shows you are the one without brains," Tork said.

The man would not let it drop. "Are you saying that because *you* are scared of him, the rest of us should be?"

Tork was up and around the fire in the blink of an eye. He drove the stock of his Sharps at the man's forehead and struck him twice more after the man sprawled flat. "Anyone else want to insult me?" he asked.

No one did.

"Did you kill him?" wondered the one in the brown hat.

"I should have," Tork said. "But all he will have is a headache to remind him to respect his betters."

Fargo had listened to enough. Carefully backing away, he turned and circled to where he had entered the lake. Dripping wet from the chest down, he tugged his boots on, then moved to the trees and slowly worked his way toward their camp. When he was again within earshot, he hunkered with his arms over his knees.

Tork's bunch were making small talk. One man told how he was wanted by the law in Texas. Another came from Missouri, where he had knifed someone in a bar fight. The gent with the brown hat related how he first met Mike Durn on a Mississippi riverboat and had worked for Durn ever since.

"He looks after his own, I will say that for Mike."

Tork revealed, "I owe him my life for the time he shot a deputy dead to keep the tin star from hauling me off to jail."

"Do you reckon all his big talk will amount to anything?" asked another. "About him running the territory, I mean? And about us having more money than we'll know what to do with?"

"All I can tell you," said the man with the brown hat, "is that he has never failed to do what he said he would."

"I like the idea of having money, Blaine," Tork mentioned. "But the part of Durn's plan I like best is rubbing out the Injuns."

"You are not fond of redskins, I take it?"

"I hate the vermin," Tork answered. "I lost an uncle and cousin to the Sioux. I kill every damn savage

101

I come across." He grinned slyly. "When no one else is around, of course."

"You must love it when Durn feeds them to his pet," Blaine remarked.

Tork and a couple of others laughed, and the former confessed, "I love it more than anything. To hear them beg and scream while they are being torn to pieces is as good as life gets."

"I wonder why men like Fargo stick up for those heathens?"

"There is no accounting for an Injun lover," Tork said. "They get on their high horse and preach as how we are all God's children and should try to get along." He burst into profanity, then said, "Try telling that to a Comanche out to lift your scalp. Or to Apaches if they get their hands on you." He swore some more. "Some folks don't have no more sense than a tree stump."

A man across from him said, "I never thought I would say this, but I have become an Injun lover, myself."

"What's that?" Tork bristled.

"I love to do those Injun gals Big Mike brings to his saloon," the man said. "Now that is my kind of Injun loving."

Hoots of laughter deflated Tork's anger. He even laughed, himself. But then he said, "Just so long as you don't decide to marry one. There is nothing worse than a squaw man."

Toward ten several of them turned in. Two more held out for another hour. Finally, only Tork and Blaine were up.

In a few minutes the small man with the big Sharps crawled under his blankets, saying, "Remember, you have first watch. Keep your eyes skinned. Wake Hank at two and have him wake Charlie at four. Tell them if all the horses aren't accounted for when I wake up, there will be hell to pay."

"You sound as if you expect them to be stolen."

"We are near Blackfoot territory, aren't we?"

The Blackfeet, Fargo well knew, had a passion for stealing horses. At one time they were the terror of the northern plains but they were not quite as hostile as in former days, in large part thanks to the tireless efforts of missionaries to convert them.

It had surprised Fargo considerably that a fierce tribe like the Blackfeet would even allow a Bible-thumper in their midst. Only time would tell if they changed their ways.

Blaine was the only one still up. For a while he stared into the fire, then he rose and stretched. His rifle in the crook of his arm, he went to the horses and made sure the tether was secure.

Fargo continued to imitate a statue. He was not ready to make his move just yet.

Blaine walked in circles around the sleepers. Dwindling flames motivated him into adding firewood, then he resumed circling. After about ten minutes he sank to his knees next to the fire and poured himself a cup of coffee. His back was to the horses.

As near as Fargo could tell, everyone else was sound asleep. Several were snoring. Tork had a blanket over his head and had not stirred since he laid down.

Fargo slowly unfurled, his Colt still in his right hand, the Arkansas toothpick in his left. The breeze had dried his buckskins enough that they did not drip as he crept toward the near end of the string. He had to exercise care that he didn't spook them. To that end, he would take a step and stop, take a step and stop, his approach slow and deliberate.

Blaine set his rifle down and sat back. He sipped coffee and uttered a sigh of contentment.

The nearest horse, a sorrel, abruptly raised its head and looked in Fargo's direction. Fargo stood still. He must not do anything the horse could construe as a threat. When it lowered its head, he advanced as before.

A second and third horse became aware of him. Both stared and pricked their ears but neither nickered.

So far, so good, Fargo told himself.

Blaine was about to take another sip. Suddenly an unnaturally loud splash out on the lake brought him to his feet with his rifle leveled. "What the hell?" he blurted. "What was that?"

Fargo wondered the same thing. The splash had been louder than a fish would make. Sometimes large animals, deer and elk and bear, went for a swim, but rarely at night, and seldom so close to a camp.

Moving around the fire for a better look, Blaine peered intently out over the water. "I don't see anything," he said aloud.

Fargo wished the man would shut up. Tork or some of the others might awaken.

"I reckon it was a fish," Blaine said. Returning to the fire, he picked up his tin cup, and squatted.

Only now he was facing toward Fargo, not away from him.

As if that were not enough, another horse raised its head and stared at the exact spot where Fargo stood. He expected it to lose interest like the others had done, but to his consternation, the horse stamped and whinnied.

14

The next instant, Blaine was on his feet with his rifle n hand. He came around the fire, glancing at the horse that whinnied and then in the direction the horse was looking.

Fargo had flattened. He was not in the circle of light yet, and he did not think Blaine could see him. He held the toothpick in front of him while easing the Colt into his holster. He would need one hand free.

Blaine stopped next to the horse and stared hard into the darkness.

None of the sleepers had stirred. One was snoring loud enough to be heard in Canada.

Fargo tensed to spring. If Blaine kept coming, he would clamp his hand over Blaine's throat and go for the jugular.

"What has you so skittish?" Blaine asked the horse. "Is something out there? A hostile? A mountain lion? What?"

Fargo noticed Blaine did not mention him. Maybe Blaine did not think he would be reckless enough to try something.

The horse lost interest and lowered its head.

"Has it gone away?" Blaine nervously asked. He lingered uncertainly, but not for long. He went back to the fire, and his coffee. Only now he sat with his back to the horses.

Within seconds Fargo reached the string. None of the animals acted up. He passed under muzzle after muzzle until he came to the Ovaro. Crouching, he reached up and cut the rope looped around the Ovaro's neck. He was about to ease up into the saddle when he had an idea that brought a grin.

Blaine was refilling his cup. He had set down his rifle.

Fargo cut a second horse free, and a third. He watched Blaine out of the corner of his eye, and when Blaine started to turn, he flattened again. But Blaine was only shifting; he did not turn all the way around. As silently as possible, Fargo cut several more horses free. He did not do the last few because they were too close to Blaine.

Fargo slid the toothpick into its sheath. Easing between the Ovaro and the horse next to it, he gripped the saddle horn and pulled himself up. The saddle creaked, but not loud enough to be heard over the snorer. He smiled as he jabbed his heels, expecting the Ovaro to explode into motion. But the stallion did not move.

Not knowing what to make of the Ovaro's refusal, Fargo slapped his legs. Again the Ovaro did not move, but the horse on the right did, nickering and shying away.

Almost immediately, Blaine swiveled at the hips and reached for his rifle. His eyes narrowed, then widened. "You!"

"Hell," Fargo said, even as he drew. He fired from the hip and the slug took Blaine high in the forehead, blowing off the top of his head.

The blast awakened the others. They scrambled up in confusion, clawing for their hardware.

Fargo fanned the Colt twice and two men dropped. So did he, over the far side of the Ovaro to the ground. He discovered why the Ovaro had not moved—it was hobbled. The rest of the cutthroats were on their feet but they had not seen him and were turning this way and that. Two of them were bent over Blaine. His fingers flying, Fargo reloaded.

"Do you see anyone?" a man anxiously asked.

Fargo sprang out. He fanned the Colt as rapidly as he could and at each shot a man crumpled. He did not spare any of them. They would kill him if they could. As the last body lay twitching and oozing scarlet, Fargo slowly straightened. He started to let out the breath he had not realized he was holding but it caught in his throat.

Tork was not among the dead. The small man had not jumped up when the rest did. Tork's blanket was exactly as it had been when he laid down and covered himself. Fargo looked closer. Draped partly over the saddle, the blanket was bunched in the middle to give the illusion a man was sleeping under it—but no one was.

Alarm rippled down Fargo's spine. He had fallen for one of the oldest ruses on the frontier. Tork had slipped out from under the blanket but left it there to give the illusion he was still asleep.

Fargo dived for the earth. He was a fraction ahead of the boom of the Sharps. A horse to his left shrieked in pain and went down thrashing.

Fargo shifted, seeking sign of Tork. But Tork, like him, was not in the ring of firelight. Fear gripped Fargo, though, as he realized that Tork *could* make out the Ovaro, as big as the stallion was, and it occurred to him what Tork might do next. Whirling, he launched himself at the saddle. But some of the horses he had cut loose were milling about, agitated by the shots and smell of blood. One was in his way. He swatted it on the rump but it did not move so he went around. As he reached the Ovaro, the Sharps thundered again and the horse he had just swatted squealed and went down.

Reining sharply, Fargo fled for the Ovaro's life. The Sharps was a single-shot rifle and it would take Tork precious seconds to reload. But God, the man was quick. Fargo barely went fifteen feet when the Sharps blasted again and invisible fingers plucked at his hat. Catching hold of the rim, he jammed it back on.

Fargo felt fleeting relief. Tork was trying to kill him,

not the Ovaro. He raced into the woods, and once he was safe, he slowed, debating whether to circle around and try to pick Tork off or to get out of there before Mike Durn or Kutler or both showed up. The decision was taken out of his hands by the pounding of hooves behind him.

Tork was after him!

Reining to the north, Fargo brought the Ovaro to a trot. He foresaw no difficulty in eluding the little killer. Weaving at random through the timber, he covered about half a mile, then drew rein to listen. All he heard was the wind in the trees. He smiled a short-lived smile.

Hooves thudded. Tork was still back there.

Fargo was impressed. Only a frontiersman of considerable ability could have kept up with him. He lashed his reins. He would have to try harder.

After at least fifteen minutes of furious riding, changing direction frequently, Fargo again stopped. The silence was reassuring. He imagined Tork's frustration at losing him, then succumbed to frustration himself when the beat of hooves told him the little man was still after him.

"How?" Fargo said out loud. He put himself in his pursuer's moccasins. Since Tork could not rely on sight, he had to be following by sound alone. And he was doing a damn good job of it.

Fargo outsmarted the bastard. Instead of galloping off and making enough noise for Tork to pinpoint where he was, he rode off slowly, and quietly, avoiding brush that might crackle or snap.

Twisting in the saddle, Fargo sought to gauge whether Tork was still following. The silence was reassuring. "I have outfoxed him," Fargo whispered to the Ovaro.

Somewhere in his wake a twig snapped.

Fargo had to hand it to him. The little man was a first-rate woodsman. And if he could not shake him off, he must try something else.

As he rode, Fargo looked for a suitable tree. Presently one appeared—a pine he could ride under, with a low branch easy to grab. Letting the reins drop, he pulled himself into the tree. The Ovaro went another ten feet or so, and stopped.

Bracing his back against the bole, Fargo clamped his legs firmly on the branch and wedged the Henry to his shoulder. He glued his eyes to his back trail, alert for movement.

The minutes passed. Two became five and five became ten and still there was no sign of Tork. Fargo grew uneasy. Something was wrong. Tork should have appeared. He shifted to scan the forest, and in doing so saved his life. A slug thudded into the trunk inches from his ear simultaneous with the boom of the Sharps.

Tork knew exactly where he was.

It left Fargo no recourse but to plunge from the branch before Tork fired again. The ground rushed up to meet him. He landed on his shoulder, as he wanted, but he did not count on the pain that shot up his right arm and the numbness that set in. Propelling himself on his other elbow, he made it behind the pine.

Fargo was mad. Not at Tork, at himself. He should have climbed higher, should have concealed himself better. He was treating Tork like an amateur and Tork was anything but. Tork was a man of the wilds, as much at home in a forest as in the saloon.

Outwitting him would take some doing.

The numbness would not go away. Fargo tried to move his right arm but he could lift it only as high as his waist. It did not feel broken or sprained, though. He suspected a nerve was pinched, and if so, the effect should wear off soon. But what was he supposed to do in the meantime with Tork out after his hide?

As wary as a mouse poking its head out of a hole in a room with a cat, Fargo eased around the trunk.

"Can you hear me, mister?"

Fargo's estimation of Tork fell. Only the rankest of greeners would talk at a time like this. "I can hear you!" he sought to keep Tork gabbing and gain time for his arm to recover.

"I hit you, didn't I? I could tell by how you fell."

"You could, could you?" Fargo wriggled his arm and opened and closed his hand.

"I would like to do you a favor," Tork called out.

"You want to surrender?"

Tork's laugh was more of a bray. "No. But I was thinking you might want to."

"And what happens when you have me in your sights? Or do we let bygones be bygones and go our separate ways?"

"You are a hoot," Tork said. "No, if you give up, I will not take you to Durn."

"You are making no sense," Fargo informed him.

"Durn would kill you slow and messy, or feed you to his pet. But me, I will do it quick and painless. Or as painless as it gets."

Fargo tried to keep the sarcasm out of his voice as he said, "You would do that for me? It is damned generous of you." He had a good idea where Tork was—in a cluster of small spruce.

"I will shoot you in the brainpan. How does that sound?"

"Oh, just dandy," Fargo said. "But I like the notion of shooting you in yours even better."

"You are not taking this serious."

"Would you like me to dig my own grave before you shoot me?" Fargo asked.

"It is a shame," Tork said. "Now we must do this the hard way."

Fargo registered movement. He had been tricked Tork had been working toward him the whole time.

Fargo flung himself back a split second before the Sharps went off. Lead thwacked the pine, nearly ripping off his cheek. Going prone, Fargo crabbed backward until he came to another tree.

Fargo's anger at himself knew no bounds. Once again Tork had nearly gotten the better of him. He must stop underestimating the little killer and be as wary as he would be of an Apache.

"Did I nick you?" Tork hollered.

Fargo was not about to fall for the same trick again

Staying on his belly, he wormed toward the Ovaro. If he could get to it without Tork catching on, he could fan the breeze and maybe give Tork the slip.

"Not answering me, huh?" Tork baited him.

A long log blocked Fargo's way. Rather than go around, he slid up and over.

"Was that you just then?" Tork called out. He was moving as he talked. "What are you up to?"

Fargo's right arm was tingling fiercely. The feeling was returning. He extended it to test it and winced at a pain in his shoulder.

The Ovaro had its head turned to one side, patiently waiting for him.

Preoccupied with his arm, Fargo crawled several yards before he awoke to the fact that the stallion was *staring* at something. Freezing, Fargo sought the reason. He spotted a vague shape flowing with remarkable agility over the ground. There was only one thing—one person—it could be.

Quickly, Fargo took aim as best he could given that he could barely see the front sight. The figure paused, and he fired. Working the lever, he went to shoot again but the figure was gone.

Heaving erect, Fargo ran to the Ovaro. Here was his chance to put some distance between him and Tork.

Wrapping his forearm around the pommel, Fargo gave a little hop and gained the saddle. He was off like a shot, which was fitting given that the Sharps let him know Tork was still alive. He headed west for half a mile then cut to the south, his intent to reach Polson before morning.

Several times Fargo stopped to listen. At last he became convinced that Tork was not after him. He slowed and wearily slumped in the saddle. He could use a few hours of sleep but it would have to wait.

His senses dulled by his fatigue, Fargo threaded through heavy timber and presently came to a broad meadow. By now he had regained the full use of his arm. Since he was not being chased, he considered it safe to cross the meadow rather than go around. But no sooner did he emerge from the trees than riders closed in from the right and the left, and gun muzzles were practically thrust in his face.

"Well, well, well," said a familiar voice. "Who do we have here?"

"Damn," Fargo said.

Kutler threw back his head and laughed.

One of the others kneed his horse up close and relieved Fargo of the Henry and the Colt.

"I did not expect you to make it so easy for us," Kutler remarked.

Fargo sighed.

"I almost feel sorry for you," Kutler said. "Mike Durn is madder than I have ever seen him. And the madder he is, the worse he likes to hurt those he is mad at. Before he is done with you, you will wish you were never born."

15

Polson was quiet and still in the hours before dawn. The clomp of hooves sounded louder than usual.

Fargo's wrists were bound in front of him. Kutler was leading the Ovaro by the reins. On either side, Kutler's men kept revolvers trained on him. He was not about to get away again.

Now, glancing over his shoulder, Kutler remarked, "I reckon you did not expect to see this place again so soon."

Fargo had intended to come back to confront Big Mike Durn, but he did not say anything.

The street was deserted save for a dog scratching itself and a pig poking about in a pile of horse droppings.

They came to a stop at the hitch rail in front of the Whiskey Mill. Kutler climbed down, looped the reins, then smirked at Fargo. "If you are waiting for a hand, you will wait until doomsday."

Fargo swung off. He was immediately grabbed by two of Kutler's men and hustled into the saloon. Evidently it stayed open all night; the bartender was wiping the bar, and at a corner table a drunk was fondling a nearly empty bottle.

"I don't know about the rest of you boys," Kutler said, "but some coffin varnish will do me right fine for breakfast."

"Food is overrated," said a string bean packing two pistols.

Fargo was propelled to the bar. As the bartender came up, he said, "I'll take whiskey. Put it on Mike Durn's tab."

Kutler and the others all looked at him, and Kutler burst out in hearty guffaws. "You beat all. Sand up to your ears."

"I'm thirsty," Fargo said.

Kutler nodded at the bartender. "Give him whatever he wants. The condemned always get a last request."

"Condemned to what?" Fargo asked. He suspected the truth but he wanted it confirmed.

"You were down below. You know what is down there."

"No, I don't," Fargo said, although he had his hunch. "I never got a look at the thing in the pit."

A grin split Kutler's face. "You will. You will look it in the eyes as it tears you to pieces."

A glass was set in front of Fargo. The barkeep sloshed whiskey over the side pouring, then moved on to the others. Cupping the glass, Fargo savored a sip that burned clear down to the pit of his stomach.

"You don't seem scared much," Kutler commented.

"It makes no sense to fret about falling from a cliff until you start to fall," Fargo said.

"You will think different once you are in that pit," Kutler said. "You will be scared as hell."

Fargo took another swallow.

Hooves drummed in the distance. Kutler turned toward the door, saying, "That will be Big Mike's or Tork's search parties."

"It won't be Tork's," Fargo mentioned. "He would be alone."

Kutler looked at him, his eyes widening. "You can't be saying what I think you are saying."

Fargo swallowed more whiskey.

"*All* of them?" Kutler said.

The others stopped talking and drinking to stare.

"Answer me, damn it. Explain yourself," Kutler demanded.

"What's to explain? Dead is dead."

"But *all* of them?" Kutler said again.

"Except for Tork, and he might be wounded." Fargo raised his glass, only to have it smacked out of his hands.

Kutler was livid. "You better be making that up. Some of those hombres were friends of mine."

"Besides," another man said, "how could you kill all of them by your lonesome?"

Fargo answered with, "Give me my Colt and I will show you."

Just then the batwings were shouldered open by Big Mike Durn. His clothes and boots were speckled with dust, and he was slapping at his jacket. Then he noticed Fargo and broke into a broad smile. "By God, you have done it, Kutler! We rode our horses into the ground hunting for him."

"It is not all good news," Kutler said.

Wending through the tables, Big Mike came to the bar. His men wearily trailed after him. "Let me hear it," he said.

Kutler explained about Tork and those with him.

Mike Durn stared at Fargo and did not say a thing. Then, without warning, he lashed out with a fist.

Hit in the gut, Fargo doubled over. He pretended the pain was worse than it was, and sagged against the bar.

Durn turned to the others. "I want four men to ride north along the lake. See if you can find Tork's camp and the bodies this bastard claims are there."

"I will go, too," Kutler offered.

"You will do no such thing," Big Mike said. "I want you here with me. You are in charge of watching over the prisoner until nightfall. I have special plans for him."

Fargo looked up from under his hat brim. Durn was not paying any attention to him. He lunged, slamming his shoulder into Durn's middle, and Durn was knocked back, stumbling against others. Before Durn could recover or anyone else could intervene, Fargo clubbed him across the jaw with his balled fists.

Durn staggered but he did not go down.

Fargo drew back his arms to hit him again but Kutler and several others pounced. He was seized in iron grips, and held fast.

"Sorry," Kutler said to Durn. "He took us by surprise. It will not happen again."

Big Mike Durn moved his jaw back and forth. "You damn near busted it," he said to Fargo.

"Let me try again and I will do better."

Durn rammed his knee up and in. Fargo caved to his knees, gasping, and saw Durn snatch a whiskey bottle from the bar and raise it aloft. "This will teach you, you nuisance!"

Kutler flung a hand between them. "Boss! Wait! If you cave in his skull, what about Caesar?"

Big Mike hesitated. The color drained from his cheeks and he slowly lowered his arm. "Thank you. I almost let my anger get the better of me. But you are right. We must not deprive my pet of fresh meat."

Fargo gathered that Caesar was the name of the creature under the saloon. He did not resist when two men, at Durn's bidding, laid hold of him.

"Take him to the storeroom. We will keep him there until the festivities. Take turns standing guard. If he escapes, Dawson, I will have you fed to Caesar along with him."

"Yes, sir." Dawson was a lank bundle of sinew who favored a riverman's cap and clothes. In a slim sheath on his right hip was a long-bladed dagger, on his other hip a Remington revolver.

They started to cart Fargo off but Big Mike stopped them, seized Fargo by the chin, and dug his fingers in. "I promise you will rue the day you stuck your big nose into my business. You might think you have been clever, killing Hoyt and the others, and burning my ferry. But all you have done is gone and got yourself dead."

"I helped Birds Landing get away." Fargo rubbed salt in the wound. "Don't forget that."

Big Mike cocked a fist but did not swing. "Damn,

you can get my goat," he said, and gestured at the men holding Fargo. "Get him out of my sight before I save Caesar the trouble."

Dawson and the other man hauled Fargo down the hall. They practically threw him in a small room and slammed the door. A key rasped, and Dawson said, "I will take the first watch. Be back here in two hours to relieve me."

"Will do."

Fargo pressed his ear to the door. He heard the jingle of the second man's spurs as he walked off. Dawson sighed, and there was a slight pressure on the door, as if Dawson had leaned against it.

From one pickle to another, Fargo thought, as he regarded his prison. The storeroom had a slit of a window high on the rear wall, barely big enough for him to slide his hand through, and barred. Shelves lined the walls from top to bottom. On some, liquor bottles were arranged in rows. On another, chips and pretzels were piled high.

Fargo's stomach growled, reminding him of how hungry he was. Since he could not think of a way to escape, he helped himself to pretzels and chips. He washed them down with blackstrap he found on a bottom shelf.

"This is a fine fix," Fargo said to himself. He gazed about the storeroom in the hope he would spot something he had missed—and he did. His curiosity piqued, he moved to the door. As was often the custom on the frontier, the hinges were made of thick leather. He ran his bound hands over them, gauging how thick they were. It could be done but he needed his hands free.

Bending, Fargo slid the Arkansas toothpick from its sheath. He reversed his grip and sliced until the rope parted. It took some doing. His fingers were sore when he was done.

Fargo examined the door more closely. It was not inset into the jamb, so his plan should work. He began cutting at the top hinge. The leather was as tough as iron. Even though he had recently honed the tooth-pick to razor sharpness, he had to press with all his might. Bit by bit the leather parted, until at last he had cut the top hinge all the way through.

Squatting, Fargo attacked the bottom one. He remembered to keep his other hand braced against the door to hold it in place, but not to press too hard or it would topple.

Unexpectedly Dawson called out, "What are you doing in there, mister?"

Fargo froze. The scritch of steel on leather had not been that loud. Evidently, Dawson had good ears. "Waiting to be fed to Caesar."

"That is not what I meant," Dawson said. "I keep hearing a strange sound."

"I was eating pretzels," Fargo said.

"No, it wasn't that. Stand back. I am going to open the door. Make a move toward me and I will put a hole in you."

Fargo thought fast. If Dawson tried to open the door with just one hinge attached, the door would tilt, warning him that something was amiss. "I was scratching at a shelf with a nail I found. Could that be what you heard?"

"What were you doing that for?"

"Something to do," Fargo said. "There is not a whole lot else."

"Well, stop it, you idiot. Twiddle your thumbs, pick your ear, I don't care what, so long as you do not make noise."

"Afraid I will dig my way out?"

Dawson laughed. "We had a girl, a Nez Perce, try to claw through the wall. She broke all her nails and tore her fingers up something awful. When Big Mike had her tossed into the pit, Caesar smelled the blood and went right for her."

When Fargo did not say anything, Dawson lapsed into silence. Fargo waited a couple of minutes, then resumed his assault on the bottom hinge. He sliced

118

slowly, wary of arousing Dawson's suspicions. As a result it took a lot longer.

Fargo lightly put his ear to the door. It was impossible to tell if Dawson was still near it or had drifted down the hall. He decided to find out. "Can you hear me out there?"

"I haven't gone anywhere."

"What is the chance of my getting a glass of water? It is stuffy in here and my throat is dry." Fargo coughed to be convincing.

"I cannot leave this spot," Dawson said. "I will have my gizzard carved out if I do."

"I won't tell if you don't."

"Leave me be."

"But I am really thirsty."

Dawson swore. "I will ask the next person who comes by to get you a glass. Now hush. Big Mike was right. You are a blamed nuisance."

Fargo carefully removed his hand from the door. It stayed upright. Backing off a few steps, he lowered his left shoulder, dug in his heels, and hurtled forward. He hit the door at a full run and it fell outward. A thud and a smothered cry rewarded his effort.

The door had crashed down right on top of Dawson. Fargo stooped and gripped the edge. They were bound to have heard in the saloon; he had only seconds in which to act.

A powerful heave, and Fargo had the door off. Dawson was on his side, his cap crumpled beside him, bleeding from a gash in his head. The Remington was under him.

Fargo would rather have his Colt, but the last he had seen of it was when Kutler took it from him at the meadow. Yells galvanized him into rolling Dawson over. Dawson groaned, but did not come around. Snagging the revolver, Fargo thumbed back the hammer just as the door at the saloon end opened.

"The son of a bitch has broken out!"

Backpedaling, Fargo shot the loudmouth as the man

was drawing. The next cutthroat flourished a six-shooter, and Fargo shot him, too.

"Stop him, damn it!" Big Mike Durn roared. "I will not be made a fool of a second time!"

Fargo wheeled and ran. He did not have cartridges for the Remington and must conserve his shots.

Behind him, gun muzzles belched smoke and lead. Ahead, a Flathead woman poked her head out of her room and promptly pulled it back again.

Fargo was eight or nine feet from the back door when it opened and another of Durn's men was framed in the doorway.

"What is all the shooting ab—?"

Fargo bowled him over with a straight arm to the throat. Then he was outside and blinking in the bright glare of the new day. For a few seconds he was blinded.

Someone seized his wrist.

16

Fargo went to strike out with the revolver but just then his vision cleared and he beheld lustrous golden hair and an hourglass shape in a pretty print dress. "Sally?"

"I heard they had caught you and was coming to help," Sally Brook said, glancing nervously at the saloon.

From deep within came a bellow of fury that nearly shook the walls. "After him, you yellow curs! After him, or by God you will answer to me!"

"Hurry!" Sally urged, taking Fargo's hand. They airly flew between the buildings and out to the main treet. Keeping in the shadows, they raced toward the millinery. Judging by the ruckus, Durn's men were pouring out the rear of the saloon and spreading out to hunt for him, but as yet none had thought to look out front.

They reached her shop. Sally quickly shut the door after them, and pulled the shades.

Fargo slipped the Remington into his holster. He looked up just as her arms encircled his neck and she pressed her cheek to his chest.

"I was so worried. Durn has been hinting at some sort of vile thing he would do to you if he ever got his hands on you again."

In brief detail, Fargo told her about the pit.

"He is an animal, that man." Sally's eyes grew moist. "I feared I would be too late and you were already dead."

Fargo had not realized she cared so much. "I am here and I am all right, thanks to you."

Sally impulsively pecked him on the cheek.

"Do it right," Fargo said, and kissed her full on the mouth. She stiffened, but then relaxed, parting her lips to admit his tongue. Her own was velvet sugar, swirling around and around in delightful arousal. "You can kiss," Fargo commented when they broke for breath.

Sally giggled. "It doesn't take a lot of talent."

Fargo begged to differ. He recollected all the women he had run across whose idea of a kiss was to have their mouth clamped tight shut. He bent to kiss her again but suddenly it was his turn to stiffen.

The din had spread to the main street. Shouts and the pounding of heavy boots warned that Durn's men were going from building to building.

Sally spun toward the door. "They will be here in a minute, and I would not put it past them to demand to search the premises."

"I will hide in the back," Fargo suggested, and turned to go.

"No." Sally held onto his arm. "If I know Durn they will look in every closet, and even under the bed. We need a hiding place they would not think to check."

"If you can find a ladder I will climb up on the roof."

"I have something better," Sally said, and pulled him toward a corner. "It is perfect."

Fargo did not know what she was getting at. In the corner stood a mannequin of some kind. The top half consisted of the carved wooden likeness of a woman; the bottom half, from the waist to the floor, was made up of wide hoops, each slightly larger than the one above it. Fine strands of wire linked them.

"I use this when I am sewing some of the dresses," Sally said as she bent and gripped the bottom hoop. A slight pull upward, and the hoops folded in on themselves. She raised them as high the mannequin's waist. "Crawl under them," she directed."

Fargo did not argue. The shouts and the pounding were louder. But there was barely enough room for him to sit with his knees tucked to his chest and his arms around his legs.

"That will do." Sally lowered the hoops. She had to push on a few to get them to go down. Then she started to a table and brought over a dress that she proceeded to slide over the top of the mannequin and down over the hoops so it hid Fargo from view. "What do you think?"

Fargo thought it was damn clever of her, and said so.

"Thanks. Now be still. I am going to open up, as I normally would, so they will not be suspicious."

Fargo heard her move off. He did not like not being able to see. Hoping she would forgive him, he drew the Arkansas toothpick, reached between the top two hoops, and cut a slit at eye level. Prying the cotton apart, he peeked out.

Sally was lifting a shade. She hung an OPEN sign on the window, then smoothed her dress and went to the opposite wall and began arranging a shelf devoted to bonnets. She had barely begun when the door was flung open and in strode Kutler and two others.

Regarding them coldly, Sally said, "What is the meaning of this? Unless you are buying something for a lady friend, you will leave this instant."

"Like hell we will, lady," one of the curly wolves said.

Big Mike Durn filled the doorway. With a swift step, he seized the offender by the front of his shirt. "You will show her the respect she is due, Adams, or you will not like the consequences."

Adams visibly paled. "Sorry, Mr. Durn. I meant no disrespect."

As an oily smile replaced his scowl, Durn faced Sally. "My apologies, my dear. Some of my associates can be most uncouth."

"Spare me the flowery talk," Sally said tartly. "You are no better than they are."

"How can you say that?" Durn said, acting stung by her remark. "Yes, I lived as a reckless riverman once. But I was born and raised on a farm in Illinois. My mother insisted I learn to read and write, and taught me manners." He paused. "But you know all that. I have shared my life's story with you."

"Yes. I know you left home when you knifed a man over a trifle, and that you fled west and wound up on the Mississippi."

"A victim of circumstance," Big Mike said.

"But I also recall you saying that you were as wild as a child as you were on the river, and as you are now," Sally said. "You constantly gave your parents a hard time. You hung a cat from the barn rafters just to see how long it would take to die."

Durn's smile disappeared. "I did not come here to discuss my past. I am searching for your friend, Mr. Fargo."

"Why bother me?" Sally said. "I have just opened up, as you can plainly see."

"So it would appear."

Sally set down a bonnet and advanced on him. "Are you calling me a liar, Mike Durn?"

"Of course not," Durn said. "But I am afraid I must insist." He snapped his fingers at Kutler and the other two and they fanned out.

"I must protest," Sally said hotly.

"Do so, my dear, by all means," Durn said. "So long as you consent to have supper with me this evening."

"You are something else—do you know that?"

Durn smiled and hooked his thumbs in his belt. "Thank you. Coming from you, I take that as a compliment."

Sally shook her head. "Honestly. When will you take the hint? There will never be anything between us."

"Never is a long time. And I can be most per—"

Fargo lost interest in their conversation. Kutler had drawn his bowie and was coming toward the manner quin. Inwardly, Fargo swore. He could not put up much of a fight, hemmed by the hoops as he was.

Durn and Sally raised their voices but Kutler paid them no mind as he stalked to within an arm's length of the mannequin and reached out with his other hand.

Fargo balanced on the balls of his feet. He would try to throw the mannequin off and leap on Kutler all in one quick movement.

"Look at what I have found!" Kutler abruptly declared. "I sure do like the yellow and the green. How much is it, ma'am?"

Both Sally and Big Mike Durn stopped arguing and glanced at Kutler in surprise.

"I beg your pardon?"

Kutler gave Sally an awkward grin. "There is this girl. I want to buy her something, and this dress is right pretty. How much is it?"

Durn looked fit to explode. "What the hell is the matter with you? We are on a manhunt and you take time to admire a silly dress?" He gestured sharply. "Find Fargo, damn it!"

Sheepishly nodding, Kutler moved toward the hall to the back, beckoning for the other two to follow.

"I will thank you not to use rude language in my presence," Sally said to Durn. "If you are going to pretend to be a gentleman, the least you can do is act like one."

"Sally, Sally, Sally," Durn said, and sighed. "I try so hard. But all you ever do is throw disrespect in my face."

"I can't help it if I am not interested," Sally said. "A woman is not always master of her heart."

"Is there someone else?" Big Mike growled. "Is that it? Tell me who, and I will have a talk with him."

Sally glanced toward the mannequin, then back at Durn. "I have not been attracted to a man in so long, I have almost forgotten what it feels like."

"Then there is still hope for me," Durn said, his smile blossoming anew. "In time you will warm to me."

"I could never open my heart to a man who forces himself on other women," Sally said. "Or do you think I haven't heard about your escapades with those poor Indian girls?"

"Rumors, my dear," Durn said. "They apply to my men, not to me. I am above that sort of thing."

"Even if I believed that, which I don't, you are as much to blame as they are. You just called them your men."

"You are nitpicking."

"If they are answerable to you, you are answerable for their actions," Sally said. "I hold you to account for all the wicked acts your men have committed."

"Wicked?" Durn scoffed, and laughed. "And which acts would those be, pray tell? Other than having some squaws come work for me?"

"You force them—"

Mike Durn reared over her. "Not *that* again! I force no one! Those squaws are working off gambling debts."

"Oh, please. You lure their fathers or husbands into the Whiskey Mill with cheap liquor. You trick them into sitting in on rigged card games. You extend credit, knowing they have no money, and when they lose, you insist they repay their debts by having their daughters or wives come work for you."

"All perfectly legal."

"But immoral, and outright wrong," Sally said.

Durn closed his eyes and pinched the bridge of his nose with his fingers. "I am beginning to think that there is no reasoning with you. You will never change your outlook."

"No, I will not," Sally said, then seemed to catch herself. "But let's say I did. Let us say I start to think favorably of you. What would you be willing to do as a token of your affection?"

Durn opened his eyes and cocked his head. "I do not follow."

"If I were to take up with you, would you be willing to let all the Indian girls go back to their villages?"

"Are you serious?"

"Never more so," Sally said. "You must have, what, close to a dozen girls in that hole you call a saloon? Give them back their lives. Send them back to their people, and I might start to think favorably of you."

"Might," Durn repeated.

"Am I not worth it?" Sally glibly asked.

"No."

Sally colored in shock. "I beg your pardon? All this talk of how much you care for me has been a lie?"

"You are mixing personal with business."

"Now I am the one who does not follow you," Sally admitted.

"It is simple," Mike Durn said. "I like you, yes, but that is personal. Those squaws are part of my business. They earn a lot of money for me. Were I to let them go, I would lose considerable income. Are you willing to take their place? To spread your legs for other men?"

Sally recoiled as if he had slapped her. "I have never been so insulted in my life! I would never stoop so low!"

"I didn't think you would," Durn said. "In which case, the squaws stay."

A strained silence fell until Sally said, "You are being honest with me, and I appreciate that. So tell me something." She paused. "You are degrading those poor women. You are stirring up sentiment against the Indians. You oppose the reservation. What's next, Mike? How far will you let your hatred of the red race drive you?"

Durn stepped to the window and gazed down the street. For a few moments Fargo thought he would not answer.

"By the end of the year I expect to have another fifty men on my payroll. The money, I should mention, will come from those squaws you are so concerned about."

"And then?" Sally prompted when he did not go on.

"I will be ready for the next step," Durn said. "I

intend to burn down the mission and have it blamed on the savages. There is nothing like a massacre to whip people up, and before I am through, every last redskin in Mission Valley, and half the territory, besides, will either be dead or driven clear to Canada."

"My God!" Sally exclaimed in horror. "I can't let that happen! I will go to the authorities and report you."

Durn turned. He was smiling again, but a sinister sort of smile. "No, you will not. Not if you want those squaws to go on living. Not if *you* want to go on living." Reaching under his jacket, he produced a revolver. The click of the hammer was ominously loud.

"You wouldn't!" Sally blurted.

"You have a lot to learn about me," Mike Durn said. And without any warning, he pointed the revolver at the mannequin.

17

Fargo was caught off guard. Somehow or other, Durn knew where he was. He started to lower his hand to the Remington but Durn's six-gun went off before he could touch it. Instinctively, fully expecting to take lead, he flinched. He felt the mannequin shake to the impact of the heavy slug followed by the patter of tiny bits and pieces raining down.

"Smack between the eyes," Durn boasted.

"What was the point of that little demonstration?" Sally angrily demanded. "You have ruined a perfectly good dress model."

"I will pay for a new one," Durn said, sliding his revolver under his jacket. "As to the point, I should think it obvious."

"At last you show your deepest, darkest nature," Sally said. "Should I go to the authorities, you will have me shot."

"No, my dear," Durn said with mock politeness, "I will shoot you myself."

Kutler and the others came out of the hall and Kutler shook his head. "No sign of him, Mr. Durn. And we looked everywhere there was to look."

"Very well," Durn said, unable to hide his disappointment. "We will keep searching." He motioned, and they preceded him out. Durn went to follow, then paused in the doorway. "I trust you will not think ill of me, Sally. I am not as cold-blooded as you must think."

"Says the man who just threatened to kill me," Sally rejoined.

"Only if you force me," Durn said. "I would rather we were intimate than enemies."

"Intimate!" Sally snorted. "It will be a cold day in Hades before that happens, I can assure you."

"We will see." On that enigmatic note, Durn departed.

Fargo was out from under the dress the instant the door closed. A walnut-sized chunk of the mannequin's head had been shot out, the shards littering the floor. "You had the right idea," he said.

"About what?" Sally absently asked. Profound sorrow etched her features.

"Reporting him. Find someone to go with you, a townsman you trust. I will give you a letter to a friend of mine, a Colonel Travis, and he will send troops."

"What about you?"

"I need to stay and keep Durn so busy he won't send anyone after you," Fargo said.

"I refuse to leave you," Sally said.

Fargo went over and put his hands on her hips and kissed her on the forehead. "Fine sentiments. But what about those Indian girls you want to save? And all those who will die if Durn pits white against red?"

Sally gnawed on her lower lip. "It might take some doing to find someone to go with me. Most everyone is too scared to do anything that might rile Mike Durn."

"There has to be someone."

"Thaddeus Thompson," Sally proposed. "Provided he isn't so drunk he can't sit a horse."

"How will you get word to him?"

"He is due in for a bottle, and he usually pays me a visit. If he doesn't show by evening, I will ride out to his cabin."

Fargo had not taken his hands from her hips and she had not objected. He made bold to pull her close and liked the pink flush that tinted her cheeks. "I admire you in more ways than one."

Grinning mischievously, Sally said, "And what ways would those be, I wonder?"

Lowering his mouth to hers, Fargo gave rein to his rising passion. She mewed like a kitten as her fingers entwined in his hair.

"Enough of those and my head will be spinning."

"We have the rest of the morning and all afternoon to ourselves," Fargo said with a wink.

Sally frowned. "Would that we did. I would have to close the shop, which might make Durn suspicious."

"You have to eat. Can't you lock up for a while at midday?" Fargo hopefully proposed.

"I do now and then," Sally mentioned. "But usually only for an hour or so."

"That is more than enough time," Fargo said, and kissed her again as added incentive. He liked how she pressed her bosom to his chest and how her fingers strayed to his shoulders and kneaded his muscles.

"My goodness. You are made of iron."

Fargo pulled back so his growing bulge was obvious. "You don't know the half of it."

Sally glanced down, and gasped. "Mercy! You have a knack for flustering me."

"The flustering has just begun." Fargo went to enfold her in his arms but she pushed against his chest.

"No. Please. As much as I want to, I expect a few customers in this morning." Sheepishly backing away, Sally smoothed her dress. "I will be back in my living quarters about noon. Wait for me in my bed if you want."

Reluctantly, Fargo repaired to the kitchen. He was famished. After firing up the stove, he checked her well-stocked pantry and helped himself to several thick strips of bacon and half a dozen eggs. He also had a hankering for a couple of thick slices of buttered toast.

The aroma set his mouth to watering.

As Fargo cooked, he pondered. There had to be a way for him to put an end to Durn's mad scheme. He considered a number of ideas, everything from sneaking back into the saloon to confront Durn to dropping Durn from afar with a rifle. That last was the safest but he had never much liked shooting from ambush.

A burp from the coffeepot let Fargo know the coffee was percolating. He had timed it so that the coffee and the food were done about the same time, and now he filled a cup to the brim and ladled heaping helpings of eggs and bacon onto a plate. Taking a seat, he rubbed his hands in anticipation and reached for his fork—and thought he glimpsed a face at the back window.

Fargo could not say for sure. The face had been there for only an instant. Pushing his chair from the table, he ran to the back door, threw it open, and almost blundered into the sunlight. Catching himself, he leaned out far enough to look in both directions. No one was in sight.

Nerves, Fargo reckoned. Returning to the table, he forked eggs into his mouth and hungrily chewed. The sizzling bacon was delicious; the toast had just the right crunch.

The hot food made Fargo drowsy. Four cups of coffee did little to help, so Fargo bent his steps to the bedroom. Not bothering to pull back the quilt, he tossed his hat on the dresser and sprawled out belly-down on the bed. It was wonderfully soft and warm.

The next thing Fargo knew, fingers were on his cheek. With a start he jerked his head up.

"Relax, silly," Sally Brook said. "It is only me."

Fargo's mind felt mired in mud and his veins were filled with turtle blood. "What time is it?" he asked, his tongue feeling as thick as a deck of cards.

"Eleven thirty. I couldn't wait. I have been thinking of you all morning." Sally's eyes gleamed with a special kind of hunger.

Fargo had slept the morning away. He shook his head to try to clear lingering mental cobwebs. "Any sign of Durn and his bunch?"

"They searched the whole town," Sally related.

"When they couldn't find you, they retired to the saloon. I haven't seen any sign of them since."

Fargo noticed she had brushed her hair and undid the top two buttons on her dress. Her notion of being brazen, he reckoned, and smothered a grin.

"Would you like me to fix you some food?"

"For some things food can wait," Fargo said. She brightened with excitement as he pulled her to him, and when he kissed her, her passion surpassed his. Her fingers roved everywhere, exploring, caressing, while her silken tongue danced a sensual waltz with his.

After a while Fargo eased her onto her side so they were face to face. He kissed and licked her neck and sucked on her ear while prying at her buttons and stays. Some dresses had a lot and hers was one. He squandered time undoing them he would rather devote to her body.

"We only have an hour as I recall," Fargo said.

"A little longer won't hurt," Sally huskily answered. "I told you I close at noon every now and then. Durn will not think it unusual."

Fargo glued his mouth to hers and silenced her for the duration. His free hand slid up over her leg and over the flat of her belly to her mounds. She was nicely endowed. He cupped and massaged each breast through her dress and felt her nipples become tacks. When he pinched one, she groaned and squirmed.

His pole was a redwood, bulging at his pants for release.

Since it was taking so long to undo her dress, Fargo hiked at the hem until he had the garment up around her thighs. He ran his palm in small circles from her knee almost to her nether mound and she grew as hot as a griddle. Her skin was creamy soft.

Inserting two fingers into her undergarments, Fargo wormed under them to her slit. Sally trembled at the contact. When he ran a finger along it to her knob, her mouth parted but no sounds came out. He stoked her furnace for a good long while but he did not enter her, not until her breasts burst free. Swooping his mouth to a hard nipple, he plunged a finger up into her.

Sally nearly came off the bed. Her mouth lavished hot kisses on his face and neck while her fingers dug at his shoulders and arms as if seeking to tear the flesh from his bones.

Fargo inserted a second finger. For a few seconds she lay perfectly still. Then she erupted into a paroxysm of release, grinding against him in abandon. Her breathing rivaled a blacksmith's bellows.

Fargo knelt between her legs. No sooner did he expose his lance than her hands were on him, fondling, cupping, doing things that brought a constriction to his throat and threatened to send him over the brink before he was ready.

Fargo aligned the tip of his sword with her sheath. Their eyes met, and he thrust in to the hilt. The bed creaked under them as they settled into a rhythm, her cherry lips forming an O of pure pleasure.

Fargo paced himself. She gushed twice, each time in a wild upheaval that added to the bite and scratch marks she was inflicting.

On they went, in and almost out. Fargo felt her inner walls contract, felt Sally spurt, and his own dam broke. Holding her hips, he pounded into her. She rose to meet each lance of his pole, willingly impaling herself in the interest of mutual release.

Coasting down from the summit was pleasant. Fargo lay in a contented haze, listening to her breathe, the damp cool of his sweat a relief from the heat of their union.

When she could, Sally whispered, "That was wonderful."

"I aim to please, ma'am."

Smiling, Sally closed her eyes, stretched, and nuzzled his shoulder. "I am so tired I can't stay awake."

"You have time for a nap," Fargo said, in the grip of lassitude he could not deny.

They drifted off.

*　　*　　*

When Fargo opened his eyes he did not know what to make of the fact the room was dark. Sitting up, he blinked in sleep-induced confusion. A glance at the window revealed night had fallen.

That couldn't be, Fargo told himself. He wondered why Sally had not woken him up, then realized she was next to him, deep in dreamland. A sense of unease gripped him as he placed a hand on her shoulder and gently shook.

"Ummmmmm?"

"It's dark," Fargo said.

Sally shifted and smiled but did not open her eyes. "What did you say?" she asked dreamily.

"It is dark out. We slept all day."

Sitting bolt upright, Sally raised her hands to her disheveled hair and gazed about the bedroom in disbelief. "Dear God! No!"

"Maybe Durn was too busy to notice," Fargo said.

"I hope you are right," Sally said, sliding her legs over the edge of the bed. "Lord, how I hope so. But he keeps such a close eye on me—" She let the thought dangle.

Fargo slid to the end of the bed and hitched at his pants. "Are all the doors locked?"

Sally nodded while pulling herself together, her worry lines obvious even in the gloom.

"If he sent someone, or he came himself, we would have heard them knock," Fargo said to ease her anxiety.

"That's right!" Sally said. "I just don't want him to find out, is all. There is no predicting what he will do." She finished dressing and lit the lamp on the end table. Holding it in front of her, she went to the door. "You can wait here if you want."

"Nothing doing."

The house was quiet. They went down the hall to the millinery, Fargo with his hand on the Remington, Sally gnawing on her bottom lip.

The store was undisturbed. Sally went to the door and tried it and smiled when she confirmed it was bolted. "I guess you are right. I am surprised, though. Mrs. Garbundy was due to come by and she is quite the busybody. She was bound to tell everyone she met that I was closed when I shouldn't be."

"I bet she ran right to Durn and told him," Fargo joked.

"I see your point," Sally said, chuckling. "I am worried for no reason."

"I wouldn't say that," said a deep voice, and from out of the shadows along the walls and from behind the counter and the mannequin came Big Mike Durn and six of his underlings, Kutler foremost among them. "I would say you have plenty to be worried about."

The rest all leveled their guns.

18

"How?" Sally Brook blurted.

"A window, my dear," Mike Durn answered. "You locked the doors but neglected to latch all the windows." He held out a hand to Fargo. "I will take that pistol, if you don't mind, and even if you do."

The ring of gun muzzles were a powerful persuader. Using two fingers, Fargo gripped the butt and slowly slid the Remington from his holster.

"Now then," Durn said, tossing the revolver to Kutler, "we can get to the matter at hand."

Sally Brook could not shake her shock. She had a hand to her throat and her eyes were saucers. "How did you find out he was here? From Mrs. Garbundy?"

"That worthless old hag?" Durn laughed. "Don't blame her. It was your own fault."

"What did I do?"

"You closed your shop. One of my men saw you hang out the closed sign. I thought nothing of it at the time. But about an hour ago I came outside for some air and saw that it was still closed."

"Oh, no," Sally groaned.

"Oh, yes," Mike Durn said, enjoying her distress. "I sent someone to snoop around. Someone who can be as quiet as a cat." He grinned at Fargo. "Someone who has a lot in common with you." Shifting toward a far corner, he beckoned. "You may come out now."

A shadow moved and assumed the form and substance of a small man carrying a big rifle. "Did you miss me?" Tork sarcastically asked.

"Took you long enough to get back here," Fargo said.

The small man came into the light and a dark stain on his shirt was visible. "Do you see this?" he hissed. "This is your doing. One of your shots glanced off a rib."

"I tried to do better."

Tork could not contain his hatred. Lunging, he drove the heavy stock of his Sharps into Fargo's ribs.

Pain exploded up Fargo's chest and he doubled over. He tensed for another blow but Big Mike Durn had caught hold of Tork's wrist.

"No more of that!"

"He has it coming!" Tork raged, trying to break free.

"And he will get his due," Durn assured him. "But in the pit, against Caesar. Think of it. You will see them torn limb from limb! Would you deprive us of the spectacle?"

It was Sally who spoke. "Them?" she repeated.

Durn let go of Tork, who stepped back but kept glaring his spite at Fargo. "Ah, yes, my dear. I am afraid you have done the one thing that would change how I feel about you."

"I don't understand."

Big Mike chuckled. "I sent Tork to look around, remember? He snuck in through the open window and saw you and your new friend asleep in your bed in a state of undress."

"Oh, God."

Fargo marveled at his own lapse. For once his keen senses had let him down, and he had not woken up.

"After all these months of courting you," Durn went on, "you go and make love to another man. I must admit I am disappointed." But more than disappointment was mirrored on Durn's face; his blazing eyes and the quirk of his jaw muscles betrayed rising

138

ury. *"You slept with another man,"* he said again, snarling each syllable.

"Please, Mike—" Sally began.

"Enough!" Durn roared, motioning for her to be silent. "I have put up with all the lies I am going to. You have deceived me for the last time." He seized her by the arm and nodded at Fargo. "Since you think so highly of him, it is only fitting that you share his fate."

"But the pit," Sally said, and shuddered. "He told me about it, told me what you do down there."

"He has spoiled the surprise," Durn said in mock disappointment, and shrugged. "Oh, well. It will still be glorious entertainment. Now all I need to decide is whether to throw you in together or one at a time."

At Durn's command, Fargo was seized by two men. Cutler and Tork covered him as they marched back to the saloon. They went the back way, and Durn was careful not to be seen.

Fargo could guess why. Throwing Indian maidens to a wild beast was one thing; a lot of whites did not care one whit about Indians. But feeding a white woman to the thing, a well-liked white woman, at that, was bound to arouse Polson's populace as nothing else could.

Sally did not say a word the whole time. She hung her head in despair, as if she had given up all hope. Fargo said her name to get her attention, and was jabbed hard in the back by Tork, who snapped at him to shut up.

The stink of the beast filled the stairwell. In the tunnel the reek was worse. As they went past the iron door with the grille, fierce snarling came through the grille.

Big Mike Durn chuckled. "Hear that? Caesar is hungry. He will feed well tonight."

Sally stirred and gazed aghast at the metal door. "What sort of beast do you keep in there?"

"Ah. So Fargo hasn't told you everything," Durn said. "What say we let you find out for yourself?"

Sudden scratching on the metal caused Sally to cringe. "This can't be happening."

Several of the men laughed.

"It's a wolverine," Fargo said.

Mike Durn stopped in midstep, and turned. "How in hell did you know that? Who told you?"

Fargo sniffed loudly several times. "The wolverine did."

"So you have encountered one before?" Durn said. "Good. Then you know what the two of you are in for. Caesar is not as big as a bear or as quick as a cougar but he is formidable in his own right."

Fargo did not doubt it. Wolverines were widely feared for two traits: their ferocity and their toughness. Legend had it wolverines even drove grizzlies from their kills, although Fargo had never witnessed it with his own eyes.

Sally was horror-struck. "Surely you wouldn't!" she appealed to Durn.

"On the contrary, my dear. You will not be the first. Well, not the first *woman*, at any rate." Durn indicated Tork. "You can thank him for how you will shortly meet your Maker. He caught the thing and brought it to me alive."

"Took some doing, too," Tork said proudly.

"He thought I might want to have it skinned and keep the hide as a rug," Mike Durn said. "But right away I saw that the monster could be put to a much better use." He beamed. "Just think. It is a foolproof way to dispose of my enemies. I have the remains hauled off into the woods, and when, as happens on occasion, those remains are found, wild animals are blamed. Usually that old bear, One Ear."

"God help us," Sally breathed.

Big Mike chortled. "I am afraid the Almighty can't hear you. He hasn't heard the others I have fed to my pet, and some of them screamed for divine help at the top of their lungs."

"Word will get out!" Sally grasped at a straw. "People will hear. They will report you to the law or the army."

"Without proof, what can the law or the army do?" Durn responded. "Besides, I only let those who work for me and a few others I know I can trust watch the feeding. They have a grand time."

They came to the oval earthen chamber at the end of the tunnel. It was empty save for the pit.

Fargo leaned over the edge for a look. Ten feet deep, with sheer sides, the bottom was stained dark in spots, the dirt furrowed with claw marks. That was not all. A fresh kill lay where the person had fallen. The face had been eaten away and not much was left of the stomach and the thighs, but Fargo knew it was the Blackfoot girl he had seen the other day.

Sally looked and turned as pale as an albino. "You can't do this to *me*," she pleaded.

"I take it you have not been paying attention," Big Mike mocked her.

"But I am *white*!"

Big Mike took a step back in feigned astonishment. "Did you hear her, Fargo? Did you hear her bare her soul?"

"I heard," Fargo said.

"What are you on about?" Sally said. "I was just pointing out that what you intend to do is foul and indecent."

"Because you are white," Durn taunted.

"Were I red or black it would be the same," Sally persisted. "It is not the skin color. It is the contemptible deed."

"Make up excuses all you want. The truth is, my dear, that when we strip away all your talk about how unfair the white man has been to the red man and how we should bend over backward for them and give them all the land they want and feed them and clothe them, you see yourself as different from them. As *better*."

"That is absurd."

"Is it?" Durn countered. "You want to save the squaws I have working for me but you are too good to share their fate."

"It is a fearful end for anyone," Sally said.

"Do you live in the same world I do?" Durn asked "The one where those heathen savages you care so much about go around killing and raping and muti lating?"

"The Flatheads have not acted up in years," Sally countered. "You can't blame them or any of the othe tribes in the region for what happened to you parents."

"Watch me," Durn declared heatedly. He ushered them around to the far side of the pit and told them to sit. "It will be a while yet, and you look haggard my former dear."

Sally slumped down, her blond locks spilling over her face.

Lowering to her side, Fargo said softly so the others wouldn't hear, "Snap out of it. We aren't dead yet."

"But we will be," Sally said, nearly in tears. "Wha chance do we have, unarmed and defenseless, agains a wolverine?"

"No chance at all if we give up before they throw us in the pit," Fargo criticized her.

Big Mike was huddled with Kutler and Tork. A length Durn and the small firebrand left, leaving Kutler and the rest to guard them. Kutler promptl strolled over, smiling happily.

"I want to thank you."

"For what?" Sally asked.

"Big Mike is so glad to finally be rid of your lover, Kutler said, nodding at Fargo, "that he is passing ou free bottles tonight. It will be the best blood and guts yet."

"The what?"

"Blood and guts. It is what we call the feeding frenzy. That damned wolverine about goes berserk."

Sally averted her face. "Please, Mr. Kutler. I would rather not hear the gory details."

"Hell, that's nothing," Kutler said. "I have seen tha critter shred flesh to ribbons and tear a throat oper clear to the jugular. It about turned my stomach watch ing him the first two or three times, but after that I got into the spirit of things."

"You are despicable, and Mike Durn is worse," Sally said flatly. "How you can live with yourself, I can't imagine."

"At least we will be breathing after tonight, which is more than I can say about you and your lover."

"That makes twice you have called him that," Sally said. "It is not entirely accurate."

"He poked you, didn't he?" Kutler leered.

Fargo was interested in an hombre over by the pit. Unless he was mistaken, that was his Colt in the man's holster.

"Must you be so crude?" Sally was asking. "Haven't I always treated you with courtesy?"

Kutler squatted a few yards away and placed his hand on his bowie. "I wouldn't call looking down your nose a courtesy. The airs you put on have not won you many friends."

"I have friends," Sally said. "In Cheyenne. In Denver. In a lot of places. Some of them will wonder when they don't hear from me. They will report me missing, and a marshal will pay Polson a visit."

"That is fine by us. Big Mike already has the story we will tell worked out." Kutler chuckled. "You sold your store and moved to California. All of us even helped load your wagon."

"That is an outright lie. No one will believe it."

"Sure they will," Kutler said. "Especially since there are people, myself being one of them who will swear on a stack of Bibles that you were always talking about moving to California one day."

Uttering a low moan, Sally bowed her head.

Kutler grinned at Fargo. "Pitiful, isn't she? You would think that at her age she would know it is dog eat dog."

"She is learning."

"I am right here!" Sally said. "I resent your talking about me as if I am some sort of simpleton."

"You are," Kutler said. "Or you would not have

143

bucked Big Mike Durn. As stupid goes, that is at the top of the tree."

A sudden burst of noise from the tunnel caused Sally to cringe and Kutler to cackle with glee.

"Hear that, missy? They are on their way. If you and your lover have any last prayers you want to say, now is the time to say them."

19

They were laughing and gay—and drinking. Bottles were passed from hand to hand and chugged like water. A number of Polson's residents mingled with Durn's lawless crew, among them a few white women. Also present, which Fargo did not expect, were the Indian women in forced servitude to Durn. He found out why when Durn cleared his throat and raised his arms to get everyone's attention.

"Tonight is a special night for me. I get rid of a thorn in my side." Durn pointed at Fargo. "I shed baggage I am better off without." He pointed at Sally Brook. "And I show you squaws what happens to those who defy me." He swept an arm at the knot of maidens, who stood off by themselves.

"Enough jawing!" an already drunk Polsonite bawled. "Let the festivities commence!"

"They will shortly," Big Mike assured him. "But first you are forgetting something."

The man blinked stupidly. "I am?"

"There won't be any festivities, as you call them, without our furry guest of honor." Durn motioned again, and half a dozen of his men hastened into the tunnel.

Fargo and Sally were to Durn's right, covered by Kutler and five others who had their guns leveled and cocked. As Kutler had put it, "One wrong twitch and we will throw you in the pit without a knee or an elbow."

Sally's hands were pressed to her bosom and she was breathing as if each breath might be her last. "What are we to do?" she mewed as the men ran off to fetch the most widely feared creature on the frontier.

"We don't give up," Fargo said.

"That is easy for you to suggest but not so easy to practice," Sally said forlornly, and dabbed at a tear forming in a corner of an eye. "Oh, Skye. I thought I was strong but I was wrong. I don't want to die."

"Who does?"

"I am so scared I could soil myself. More scared than I have ever been in my whole life."

"I will need your help when the time comes," Fargo said.

"I don't see what use I can be," Sally responded. "We can't fight the thing. Hands and feet are no match for teeth and claws."

"You might be surprised." Fargo noticed Tork give him a look that suggested the end could not come soon enough to suit him. Fargo smiled at him and he flushed red.

"How can you be so calm?" Sally asked, wringing her hands. "A person would think you were fed to wild beasts all the time."

"When you have survived Apaches, sandstorms, and blizzards," Fargo said, "a wolverine is no more than a nuisance." He was trying to get her to relax but she was too overwrought.

"How can you jest at a time like this? I am telling you, my blood is water. My legs are shaking so bad, if I try to take a step I will collapse."

Kutler heard her, and said, "Don't worry on that score, missy. You won't need to walk to the pit. We will carry you over and throw you in."

"Doesn't it bother you, being so unspeakably evil?" Sally retorted.

"Not at all," Kutler said. "That is the thing people like you can never seem to savvy."

"People like me?"

"Those who go around doing good, who think virtue is everything. Your kind always think everyone else is the same as you." Kutler shook his head. "But it doesn't work that way, lady. I don't have a sliver of virtue anywhere in me, and I am happy I don't. I look out for me and me alone. The rest of the world can go hang itself."

"You are just saying that to upset me," Sally said. "There must be a kernel of decency deep down inside of you."

"See what I mean?" Kutler said, and laughed. "You go through life with blinders on."

"I am not an infant," Sally said archly.

Kutler glanced at Fargo. "You would think that someone so pretty would not be so dumb."

His insults had taken Sally's mind off the pit, and her fears. "If you were not holding that gun on us, I would claw your eyes out."

"Speaking of claws," Kutler said, and bobbed his chin at the tunnel.

They were coming. Six men holding the ends of long poles that had been slid between the bars of a large wooden cage. Inside the cage, snarling and spitting and biting at the bars, was the scourge of the Rockies. Between the beast's moving about, and the heavy cage, it was all the men could do to carry their burden without falling.

"Caesar!" Big Mike Durn said fondly.

Sally Brook shuddered.

A hush fell over the spectators. Every neck craned for a better look at the cage. One woman squealed in delight and cried out, "Oh! Isn't he positively vicious!"

A path was cleared. As the cage went past them, many backed away in terror.

The animal that instilled such potent fear was oblivious to the effect its presence caused. It was snapping at a bar, its razor teeth flashing.

Sally's hand found Fargo's. "I will faint," she said weakly. "I swear I will pass out."

"Be ready to do exactly as I tell you, when I tell you," Fargo said. "We will only get one chance."

"At what?" Sally's desperation was climbing.

Fargo didn't answer. Not with Kutler and the others right there.

The cage was deposited at the edge of the pit. Ropes were produced and fastened to the ends of the poles. Then, with ten men straining and sweating, the cage was carefully lowered to the bottom.

The wolverine stopped biting the bars. It had been through this before. It knew what came next.

Durn walked to the edge. A man handed him a long rawhide cord that was tied to the top bar at one end of the cage. Gripping the cord firmly in both hands, Durn tugged.

The end of the cage rose.

Cheers broke out as Fargo at last had a clear look at the creature he was about to tangle with.

Gluttons, they were called. Skunk bears was another name. They were bulky like bears, but where a full-grown black bear might weigh over five hundred pounds and a full-grown grizzly might top the scales at over a thousand, a large male wolverine—and this one was large—weighed a paltry fifty pounds.

But what wolverines lacked in weight they made up for in ferocity. No other animal was as fierce—not grizzlies, not wolves, not mountain lions. Savagery incarnate, wolverines were immensely powerful. Pound for pound, they were the strongest creatures on the continent. Add to that teeth like knives and claws like sabers, and their reputation was justly deserved.

This one had a typical dark brown coat with yellow splashes across its shoulders and over its hips, and lighter coloration above its eyes and along the edges of its ears.

The stink was abominable. Wolverines, like skunks, emitted a foul musk, which they used to mark caches of food and discourage other predators. But they also emitted the musk when they were excited, like now.

"Caesar!" Mike Durn called, and the wolverine

looked up. "Do you see, Fargo? He knows what we call him. Wonderfully clever, these things."

That was another of their traits. Wolverines were notoriously shrewd. They deprived trappers of their livelihood by raiding traplines, going from trap to trap and ripping apart the animals that were caught. Or they would come on a camp high in the mountains, and in an unguarded moment, wreak havoc by tearing articles to shreds and generally disporting themselves as if they were the devil in four-legged guise.

Caesar had commenced to prowl about the pit and irritably growl and snarl at the excited onlookers.

A man more tipsy than most nearly plummeted over the edge when he was bumped by a friend, and instantly the wolverine bounded to a spot directly below him, eager to feed on human flesh.

"Look at him!" Durn gushed in admiration. "Did you ever see anything so savage? A brute in every sense of the word."

Sally was appalled. "That thing is a fiend, yes, but at least it has an excuse."

Durn turned on her, his good mood evaporating. "Explain that remark, my dear."

"That wolverine can't help itself. Yes, it is savage, but it is merely being true to its nature. It was born as it is and can be nothing other than itself." Sally did not keep the contempt from her voice as she went on. "But you, on the other hand, are a true abomination. You were not born as you are. You choose to be sadistic instead of kind. You lord it over others because you want to. You kill because you delight in spilling blood. The wolverine is not the monster here. You are."

"At last you understand me," Big Mike said.

"I have always understood," Sally replied. "Why do you think I rebuffed your advances time and again? Your pretense did not fool me."

Durn said nothing.

"You are a common thug, nothing more," Sally unleashed more barbs. "A river rat who left the river but is still a rat, nonetheless. Oh, I will grant you are a notch above the rest of your breed, in that you can read and write, and have a certain coarse intelligence. But you have your delusions as well. Above all, you have your hate, and it is that which will destroy you."

Fargo was as amazed as Mike Durn at her outburst. He tensed to protect her should it be necessary.

But Durn did not fly into a rage. Instead, he laughed heartily, then said, "I swear. That was some speech. But you can come down from your pedestal now. The fun is about to begin."

Those assembled fell quiet when Big Mike bellowed for silence. Smiling broadly, he regarded their expectant faces. "Tonight you are in for a special treat. Special because my pet will feed more than once. Special because a white woman is one of the morsels. Special, too, as an object lesson."

"A what?" someone asked.

"When I give an order, I expect it to be obeyed. When it isn't, there are consequences." Durn swung toward a group of his men. "Mr. Dawson, step forward, if you please."

Fargo remembered the lanky riverman who had guarded him in the tunnel, and guessed what was coming.

Dawson's surprise rooted him in place, but only until Durn motioned and several others pushed him forward. His dagger was snatched from its sheath, and his Remington, which had been returned after Fargo was caught, was lifted from his holster. It all happened so rapidly, he was disarmed and standing before Durn before he could collect his wits.

"Anything to say?" Mike Durn asked.

Licking his thin lips, Dawson croaked, "What is this? I am not one of them." He nodded toward Fargo and Sally.

"You have forgotten."

"Forgotten what?" Dawson asked, his voice rising.

"I set you to keep watch over Fargo," Durn jogged

his memory. "I warned you that if he got away, I would feed you to Caesar."

"But that was just talk," Dawson said. "To scare me so I would take you serious and not doze off."

"I do not make idle threats."

Dawson glanced into the pit, and swallowed. "Now hold on, Mr. Durn. Don't I always do as you want, no questions asked? I couldn't help it if he pushed a door on top of me."

"Did you think to search him before he was put in the storeroom?" Mike Durn asked.

"No. But I was just doing what you told me to do. You should have searched him yourself if—" Dawson stopped, petrified by his blunder.

"So it is my fault Fargo got away?"

"No, no, no," Dawson bleated. "I am not saying that. I am not saying that at all."

"It sounded like you were to me."

Dawson started to back away from the pit. "You can't!"

All it took was a quick step and a hard shove. Mike Durn was smiling as he pushed Dawson over the edge, his smile widening at the shriek that filled the pit.

Sally turned away and covered her ears with her hands.

Not Fargo. He watched the wolverine, studying its movements. It was on the other side of the pit when Dawson went over. At the *thud* of Dawson hitting the earth, the beast whirled. Dawson, terrified, scrambled to his hands and knees, whining, "Not this! Not this! Not this!"

Most everyone else was pressing forward for a better view, including the white women, whose faces gleamed with bloodlust. The Indian women, though, hung back, their distaste transparent.

With a loud snarl, the wolverine streaked across the pit. Dawson let out a shriek. He was so petrified, he made no attempt to fight back when the wolverine sprang. At the last instant he raised his hands in front of his face, a futile bid to ward off the inevitable.

151

The wolverine bowled Dawson over. The riverman screamed as its teeth sheared through his outspread fingers and tore into his neck. The scream faded into a wet, bubbly gurgle, and then died entirely as his throat was ravaged. His body convulsed a few times and was still.

The wolverine did not stop there. In a mad frenzy, it slashed and tore and bit until Dawson's face and neck and chest were a ruin of mangled flesh and pooling blood.

Big Mike Durn laughed for joy, and turned to Fargo and Sally Brook. "I hope you two were paying attention. Your turn is next."

20

Whoops of glee and laughter greeted Dawson's demise. If any of Mike Durn's men objected to one of their own dying, they did not let on out of fear that what happened to Dawson could happen to them. As for the rest of the onlookers, it was wonderful fun. One of the women commented on how she wished there had been more blood. A man remarked that Dawson had not screamed nearly as much as he thought Dawson would.

Fargo was more interested in Sally. She was quaking like an aspen leaf, her fists clenched so hard her knuckles were white. When he touched her shoulder, she nearly jumped out of her skin. Leaning over, he said in her ear, "You must stay calm."

"How, in God's name? I am not you. You have probably witnessed things like this before."

Fargo had. Animal attacks were common in the wild, and the wilds were his home. But that was not the issue. "I need you to be brave," he stressed.

"You ask the impossible," Sally said, shaking her head. "I will pass out when Durn pushes us in, and that will be that."

"Try not to," Fargo urged.

"But I *want* to," Sally said. "I would rather be unconscious when that thing pounces. I won't feel the pain. I won't experience the horror."

"It is not as hopeless as you think," Fargo said. Then, making sure Durn had his back to them, and that neither Kutler nor Tork were listening, he whispered, "I have my knife."

"So?" Sally said. "What good will it do us? You might as well throw pebbles at it."

"Trust me," Fargo said. "I know what I am doing. I have a plan." A crazy plan, a plan fraught with peril, a plan that could as easily get him killed as anything, but a plan, nonetheless.

"Do we make a break for it before they throw us in?"

"No." Fargo doubted they would reach the tunnel.

"Oh! You intend to kill Durn! And then we can escape in the confusion." Sally grinned, thinking she had figured it out.

"There will be confusion, yes," Fargo said. But not for the reason she expected.

Sally put her lips to his ear, her breath warm on the lobe. "When do we make our break?"

"After they throw us into the pit."

"After?" Sally blinked. "Are you insane? Once we are in that pit, we are as good as dead."

"Listen to me," Fargo said, and gently squeezed her arm to soothe her. "When we go over the side, try to land on your feet. Stay close to me and keep your back to the wall. I will take care of the rest."

"If only I could believe that."

Fargo leaned closer. "There is one thing more you can do," he said, and told her what it was.

Sally drew back, her wide eyes fixed on his. "You *are* insane."

"It will work," Fargo promised.

"Listen to yourself. It is a wolverine, not a dog or a cat. And ten feet is awful high."

"I am counting on the wolverine to help," Fargo said. "And remember, it doesn't weigh more than sixty pounds."

"That is plenty enough," Sally said.

Then there was no more time to talk. Durn's men seized them and hauled them to the edge but did not, as yet, hurl them over.

Mike Durn had some crowing to do. He raised his

154

arms. "Friends! Now for some real fun! Two at once, and one of them a white woman!"

Not one of the faces ringing the pit was sympathetic to their plight. Which made it easier for Fargo; he had no qualms about what he was about to unleash on them.

"You squaws over there!" Durn said. "Pay attention! This could be you if you don't do as I say!" He stepped around behind Fargo and Sally and placed a hand on their backs between their shoulder blades. "And so it ends."

"Remember," Fargo said to her.

Mike Durn paused. "Remember what?"

"That you are a miserable son of a bitch who will get what he has coming to him," Fargo predicted.

Always quick to anger, Durn swore and shoved.

Fargo didn't resist. He kept his legs under him as he dropped, his arms out from his sides. Beside him, Sally screamed, her fingers plucking at his sleeve. He came down hard on his boot heels and pitched backward. He thrust his hands behind him and came up against the wall. From above came liquor-spawned hoots and cries of derision as he turned and nearly tripped over Sally, who was on her knees, staring straight ahead with her features frozen in shock.

The wolverine was slinking toward them.

"Get up!" Fargo commanded, and yanked her off the ground. "Remember what I told you."

Sally numbly nodded, saying in dread, "I don't know if I can."

"If you can't we are dead." Fargo would give a good account of himself with the toothpick, but he had no illusions about the outcome.

Its blunt snout thrust out, the wolverine slowly advanced. It kept glancing from Sally to Fargo and back again as if it could not make up its mind which one it would attack first.

"Be brave!" Fargo cautioned. He sidled away from her, his back to the pit wall.

The wolverine stopped. Its muzzle and face were

spattered red with Dawson's blood and a strip of pink flesh hung by a shred from its bottom teeth. Snarling, the beast snapped at the air.

Sally whimpered and made as if to press back into the wall. "I can't do this!"

Fargo did not respond. It was essential the wolverine focus on her and only on her.

"Oh, God, oh, God, oh, God, oh, God!" Sally wailed.

The wolverine had taken a step. Now it took another, its head low to the ground the way a bear's would be when a bear was about to attack. It glanced once at Fargo, apparently decided he did not pose a threat, and continued toward terror-struck Sally.

The cries from on high were at a fever pitch. The onlookers were thirsting for more blood to be spilled. They reveled in the prospect of witnessing another gory death—so long as it was not their own.

Fargo halted and glanced up. Mike Durn and Kutler were whooping as loud as everyone else. But not Tork. The little man was still, his brow knit. Evidently Tork suspected he was up to something.

The wolverine crouched and growled, about to charge.

Coiling his legs, Fargo did the last thing anyone expected. He rushed at the wolverine. The instant he exploded into motion, Sally did what she was supposed to do—she screamed at the top of her lungs to keep the wolverine's attention on her.

It worked.

Fargo had only six feet to cover, and then he was behind the wolverine. Wrapping a hand around each hind leg, he wrenched them off the ground. At the contact the wolverine twisted and bit at him and sought to reach him with its claws. But Fargo had already started to spin, and as he turned, the wolverine's front legs came off the ground, too.

Fifty pounds was no feather but it was nowhere near the heaviest Fargo could lift. He swung the enraged glutton in a circle, and kept on swinging. Faster and aster, straining harder and harder, he whirled like a top, his shoulders bearing the strain, his whipcord body taut.

Some of those above broke into laughter. They did not divine his purpose.

The wolverine was trying with all its feral might to get at Fargo's hands but could not reach them. Its rage was boundless.

Came the moment toward which Fargo had been building. He was swinging the wolverine as fast as he could, its body as high off the ground as he could raise it without losing his balance. On his next swing, he lowered the beast's bulk higher still and let go at the apex of his swing. The wolverine shot toward the rim.

The result was everything Fargo hoped for.

The creature did not quite reach the top and started to fall back, but it was so near that it caught hold of the earthen wall with its long claws and by furiously pumping all four legs, clawed its way up and out.

For a few heartbeats the tableau was frozen as the astonished onlookers and the enraged wolverine were eye to eye. Then the wolverine did what wolverines were famed for doing—it went berserk. With the closest to a roar Fargo heard it utter, the beast was in among the throng, slashing and tearing in a whirlwind of slaughter. Women and many of the men screamed and screeched and fled in panic, pushing and shoving one another in their bid to escape.

Fargo lost sight of Mike Durn in the melee. He ran to Sally and took her hand. "It worked! Come on!" he shouted to be heard above the bedlam.

"But how will we get out of this hole?" she wanted to know.

For an answer, Fargo pulled her toward the cage.

Above them the carnage continued, the wolverine slaying and maiming with dervish abandon. Here and there a few men had the presence of mind to try and use a gun but could not shoot for the press of bodies. One man did squeeze off a shot, but the slug meant for the wolverine instead blew a hole in the thigh of another man who went down in the wolverine's path and was promptly dispatched with a raking swipe of its claws.

What happened next, with all the pushing and shoving, was inevitable. Two men came hurtling over the edge and fell hard to the bottom. Fargo reached them before they could rise. Both wore revolvers, which he snatched from their holsters. As he straightened, a rifle thundered and lead splatted the dirt.

Fargo glanced up.

Smoke was curling from the muzzle of Tork's Sharps. The little man swore and swooped a hand to his hip.

Fargo fired both revolvers.

The impact jolted Tork back a step. He stared at the twin holes in his chest, then down at Fargo, and said something that was drowned out by the pandemonium. Dropping the Sharps, he oozed into a heap.

Fargo turned. The two men who had fallen into the pit were starting to get up. He dissuaded them with a wag of the pistols. Then, motioning to Sally, he ran to the cage. "Wait until I am out, then climb on top."

Wedging the revolvers under his belt, Fargo clambered up. The cage was sturdily built to prevent the wolverine from breaking out and easily bore his weight. Since it was four feet high, once he straightened, it was simplicity itself for him to jump and catch hold of the rim.

The chamber had gone quiet save for whimpers and moans and a sucking sound. From the tunnel came screams and curses mixed with the snarls and growls of the wolverine.

Fargo pulled himself up so he could see over the edge. He counted seven sprawled forms: one a woman lying in a spreading scarlet pool, another a man whose torn throat bubbled and frothed.

Digging his toes into the dirt wall, Fargo levered up and out. He promptly drew one of the revolvers, and turned, but the two men in the pit had behaved themselves and were standing well back from Sally.

Lying flat, Fargo offered his other hand to her. She had already climbed on the cage, and it was the work of a moment for him to pull her up beside him.

"We did it! We actually did it!" Sally happily marveled. Then she noticed the dead and dying, and sobered. "What now?"

"You stay here. I have some killing to do."

Fargo made for the tunnel. The wolverine had lived up to its reputation, and then some; he stepped over body after body. A few had been trampled in the panic and did not bear a single scratch or bite mark.

The iron door with the grille hung partly open. Fargo was almost past it when a slight sound caused him to spin.

Kutler was almost on him, the bowie raised to stab.

Fargo fired, stepped back as Kutler sliced at his neck, fanned a second shot, stepped back again as Kutler speared at his stomach, and fanned yet a third.

Each jarred Kutler, the last keeling him against the door. He never said a word. He simply smiled a wistful sort of smile, the bowie fell from fingers too weak to hold it, and he melted, his eyes already glazing.

Fargo went faster. It seemed to take forever to climb the stairwell. In the narrow confines, with each step jammed by the panicked herd of humanity fighting to reach the top, the wolverine had wreaked havoc.

Only two bodies were in the hall. Fargo cautiously peered out the back door and glimpsed a hairy form loping toward the distant mountains.

Behind Fargo, a revolver crashed. Lead bit into the jamb as Fargo whirled and responded in kind. At the other end of the hall, Big Mike Durn staggered but fired again.

Fargo dropped the revolver he had emptied and drew the other one. He slammed shot after shot, emptying the second six-shooter into Durn's chest and face.

The man who would be lord and master of Flathead country died on his feet, pink fluid oozing from a hole between his eyes.

Then Sally was there, hugging him. Fargo draped an arm across her slender shoulders and started toward the saloon. "I can use a drink. How about you?"

An impish grin curled those luscious lips. "I have a better idea. Let's take a bottle to my place and make more use of that bed of mine."

Fargo grinned. "Woman, you are a hussy at heart."

"Is that a yes or a no?"

Smacking her on the fanny, Fargo chuckled. "What do you think?"

LOOKING FORWARD!
The following is the opening
section from the next novel in the exciting
Trailsman series from Signet:

**THE TRAILSMAN #322
APACHE AMBUSH**

*The Territory of New Mexico, 1861—
a hotbed of hate and greed.*

Skye Fargo had a bad feeling about the place.

It was named Hot Springs. It was not much of anything except a few cabins and shacks and the inevitable saloon. Then, over the hot springs, there was a structure that reminded him of a Navajo hogan, only it was the size of a small hill.

Fargo wanted a drink and a meal he did not cook himself, so he rode down the short, dusty street to the hitch rail in front of the saloon and stiffly dismounted. He had been in the saddle since daybreak, and here it was almost sundown.

Tall and broad of shoulder, Fargo wore buckskins, a hat that had once been white but was now dust brown, and a red bandanna. Women were fond of his

161

ruggedly handsome face. Men who had heard of him were wary of his fists and his Colt. Stretching, he sauntered into the saloon. After the harsh glare of the sun it took a few seconds for his eyes to adjust to the gloom. He paid no attention to the customers at the tables but walked right to the bar, smacked it loud enough to get the bartender to start in his direction, and demanded, "Whiskey."

If there was anything better for soothing a dry throat, Fargo had yet to find it. He drained his first glass at a gulp and motioned for more, then decided to hell with it and paid for the bottle. Taking it to a corner table, he sank down with a sigh and prepared to get pleasantly soused. He frowned when two pairs of boots came toward his table, and looked up to see who filled them.

The one on the right was short and thin; he had eyes an owl would envy. He was dressed in a costly store-bought suit, and his boots had been polished to a fine shine.

The one on the left was muscle, and a lot of it. Over six feet and over two hundred and fifty pounds, if Fargo was any judge. This one wore a well-used shirt and pants, and his boots were scuffed. The scars on his knuckles gave warning his hands were not ornaments.

"Go away," Fargo said.

Both men stopped and the owl blinked in surprise. "You have not heard what I have to say."

"I don't want to hear it," Fargo set him straight. "Go away."

"I am afraid I can't," the owl said. "I am Timothy P. Cranmeyer of the Cranmeyer Freight Company."

Fargo was amused. "You named your company after yourself?"

"A common enough practice," Cranmeyer said amiably. "But that is neither here nor there. We need to talk."

"No, we do not," Fargo said as he filled his glass.

"I cannot say I think much of your attitude. I am an important man in these parts."

Fargo snorted.

Cranmeyer colored, then jerked a thumb at the muscle next to him. "This is Mr. Krupp. He works for me. He is the captain of my freight train."

"Good for him," Fargo said, a bit testy now that the man would not take the hint.

The muscle spoke. "I make sure people show Mr. Cranmeyer the respect he deserves."

Fargo's hand came up from under the table holding his Colt. He set it on the table with a loud *thunk*. "Here is your respect, Cranmeyer. Take your pet bear and go annoy someone else."

Amazingly, Timothy P. Cranmeyer did no such thing. "You will hear me out whether you want to or not. It is in your own best interest."

Skye Fargo sighed. "If there is one thing this world does not have a shortage of, it is idiots."

"You look as if you can handle yourself in a scrap, and I have need of men to help guard my freight wagons. They are bound for Silver Lode up in the Mimbre Mountains and will be here by noon tomorrow. I rode on ahead."

"Good for you," Fargo said, and drained half the glass. "I am not interested."

"I will pay you sixty dollars for two weeks' work," Cranmeyer persisted. "You must admit that is good money."

That it was, but Fargo had a full poke. "I am still not interested. I am on my way north, not west."

"The Fraziers are driving the wagons," Cranmeyer said, as if that should mean something.

"Mister, I do not care if the president, the pope, and the queen of England are driving. You are a nuisance. Skedaddle, and be quick about it. My patience has flown out the window."

Krupp's voice was as deep and low as a well. "Do

you want me to teach him some respect, Mr. Cranmeyer?"

Fargo placed his hand on his Colt. "Be my guest. I have not shot anyone in a few days and am out of practice."

Showing no fear, Krupp balled his big fists. "Are you so yellow you can't do it without that?"

"There is an epidemic of stupid," Fargo said, then flicked his Colt up. At the blast, Krupp's hat did a somersault and flopped to the floor between the two men. Krupp stood there as calm as could be, but Cranmeyer started and took a step back.

"You are awful quick on the trigger."

"Only when I am mad, and thanks to you, I am mad as hell." Fargo pointed the Colt at him. "For the last time. Make yourself scarce or you will have to make do without an ear."

"I do not think much of your manners," Cranmeyer said stiffly.

"I don't give a good damn whether you do or you don't. I will count to ten and then the perforating begins." Fargo paused, then began his count. "Four. Five. Six. Sev—"

"Hold on. What happened to one, two, and three?"

"They flew out the window with my patience." Fargo resumed his count. "Seven. Eight. Ni—"

"All right. All right." Cranmeyer held up both hands. "I am leaving. But if you change your mind I will be in Hot Springs until about two tomorrow afternoon. That is when I hope to leave for Silver Lode."

Fargo did not hide his surprise. "You *still* want to hire me?"

"I told you. I need men who are not trigger shy, and anyone who will shoot me over a trifle will more than likely not mind shooting Apaches and anyone else who might give me trouble."

Despite himself, Fargo laughed. "Look, Cranmeyer. I do not need the money. And I am not in the mood to tangle with the Mimbre Apaches. I have done it before and been lucky to get away with my hide."

"I thought so," Cranmeyer said, and smiled. "You look like a man who is more wolf than sheep."

"Save the flattery. I still won't go."

"Did I mention the Fraziers are driving three of the wagons? That is usually enough to entice most."

"Why in hell would I care who the drivers are? Muleskinners interest me about as much as head lice."

Now it was Cranmeyer who laughed. "I take it you have never heard of the Fraziers, then?"

"Should I?"

"Word has gotten around. You see, as muleskinners go, they are special in that they are females. Sisters, no less, with a reputation for being as wild and reckless as can be."

Fargo was genuinely surprised. Muleskinning was hard, brutal, dangerous work. He had only ever met one other woman who did it for a living, and she had the misfortune to be born a man in a woman's body. "I am still not interested." He was, however, curious.

"Very well. I tried." Disappointed, Cranmeyer turned. "Come along, Krupp. We will see if there is anyone else we might hire. I must replace the three who quit on me or we will not have enough protection when we start up into the mountains."

Krupp, scowling, picked up his hat.

Fargo could not resist asking, "Why did they quit on you?"

Cranmeyer looked back. "One of them tried to take liberties with Myrtle Frazier and she took a whip to him. It embarrassed him, being beaten by a woman. He quit, and his friends left with him."

"So you weren't kidding when you said these women are wildcats."

"Mister, you have no idea. If they weren't three of the best muleskinners in all of the Territory of New Mexico, I would have nothing to do with them. At times they can be almost more trouble than they are worth.''

Fargo took a sip. He had not been with a woman in a while, and if there was one thing he could not do without, besides whiskey, it was women. He had half a mind to look up the Frazier sisters when the freight wagons arrived. But if Myrtle was any example, all he would get for his interest was the lash of her bullwhip. He shrugged and decided to forget them.

Before long the sun set and some of the citizens of Hot Springs, a paltry dozen or so, drifted into the saloon to indulge in their nightly ritual.

The bartender turned out to be the owner, and he turned out to have a wife who was also the cook. Fargo ordered a thick slab of steak with the trimmings and a pot of coffee to wash the food down. He was halfway through the steak, chewing a delicious piece of fat, when a new arrival perked his interest. She was young and saucy and had curly red hair, and she sashayed into the saloon as if she had the best pair of legs a dress ever clung to. The locals grinned and greeted her warmly, and in return received pats on the back or the backside or, in a few cases, a peck on the cheek. She handed her shawl to the bartender, gazed about the room, blinked, and came strolling over to Fargo with her hands on her hips and an enticing grin on her lips.

"Well, what do we have here? You are new. Are you staying a spell or just passing through?"

"The only way I would stay more than one night is if I was six feet under," Fargo said.

"Hot Springs isn't *that* bad," the vixen replied, chortling. "But I will admit that there is not a whole lot to do around here except sit in the hot spring and sweat."

Fargo showed his teeth in a roguish smirk. "I can think of another way to work up a sweat, and it is a lot more fun than sitting in scalding hot water."

She looked him up and down, and nodded. "I

reckon you could, at that." Offering her hand, she said, "I am Tilly Jones. Do you have a handle or do I just call you Good-Looking?" She let the clasp linger and when she pulled her hand back, she slid her middle finger across his palm.

Fargo was interested. He needed something to do until dawn and she would do nicely. Quite nicely, in fact. "What time do you get done here?"

"My, oh, my," Tilly grinned. "You could at least introduce yourself. Or are you a randy goat who only thinks of one thing?"

"I am no goat," Fargo said. "But I still think of that one thing a lot." He introduced himself.

"Right pleased to make your acquaintance." Tilly pulled out a chair. "How about if you buy me a drink, or I will have to go to talk to someone else. Sam over yonder isn't happy unless I am making him money."

A wave of Fargo's arm brought the bartender with an extra glass. He filled it and watched with admiration as she swallowed half. "You have had red-eye before."

Laughing, Tilly smacked her delightfully full strawberry lips. "More times than either of us can count. I dare say I can drink most any man here under the table."

"You are welcome to try," Fargo challenged.

Swirling the whiskey in her glass, Tilly replied, "Don't think I wouldn't. But if we are to have a frolic later I best stay sober." She glanced at the batwings, worry in her emerald eyes, and bit her lower lip.

"Something wrong?"

"Oh, nothing I can't take care of. This gent strayed in about a week ago and took a shine to me, and the next thing I knew he was following me around like a little calf, making cow eyes and saying as how the two of us were meant for each other."

Fargo chuckled. Some people equated passion with love. A silly notion, but then a hunger for a female had made many a man do damned silly things.

"It is not all that humorous," Tilly said. "He has gone from being an amusement to a bother I can do without." Suddenly she stiffened and her hand rose to her throat.

The batwings had parted and in marched a rail-thin apparition with a bushy beard, a tangle of black hair, and a nose like a hawk's beak. His dirty clothes and the pick wedged under his belt marked him as a prospector. He had to be in his middle twenties. He spotted Tilly and strode over, shoving aside two men who were in his way.

"Here you are."

"Go away, Stein. I am working."

Ignoring Fargo, Stein gripped her arm and tried to pull her to her feet, but she resisted. "I don't care what you are doing. You have put me off long enough. I am taking you back up into the mountains with me."

"Like hell you are," Tilly said.

"I will not take no for an answer." Stein tugged on her again with the same result. "The sooner you get it through your pretty head that from now on you are mine and only mine, the better off you will be."

"Leave me alone!" Tilly snapped. "Or I'll go to the law and file a complaint."

"What law?" Stein scoffed. "The nearest tin star is hundreds of miles away." He gripped her chin. "On your feet."

Fargo had witnessed enough. Sliding his chair back, he came around the table and put his hand on Stein's shoulder. "The lady doesn't want your company. Light a shuck while you still can."

Stein straightened and pushed Fargo's hand off. "I don't take kindly to meddlers, and I take even less kindly to being told what to do." He slid the pick from under his belt. "You are the one who will make himself scarce, or by the eternal, I will cave in your damn skull."